Up Pops the Devil

Up Pops the Devil

Lachá M. Scott

URBAN
CHRISTIAN

Urban Books, LLC
97 N18th Street
Wyandanch, NY 11798

ISBN 13: 978-1-62286-822-3
ISBN 10: 1-62286-822-6

First Trade Paperback Printing December 2015
Printed in the United States of America

10 9 8 7 6 5 4 3 2 1

This is a work of fiction. Any references or similarities to actual events, real people, living or dead, or to real locales are intended to give the novel a sense of reality. Any similarity in other names, characters, places, and incidents is entirely coincidental.

Distributed by Kensington Publishing Corp.
Submit Orders to:
Customer Service
400 Hahn Road
Westminster, MD 21157-4627
Phone: 1-800-733-3000
Fax: 1-800-659-2436

Up Pops the Devil

by

Lachá M. Scott

Acknowledgments

Thanks to God first and foremost for birthing the gift of writing in me.

Thank you to my daughters, Jasmin, RhonShay, and ShayLa, for allowing me to do what I do by sharing me with my readers, within the ministry, and amongst the various engagements I partake in to share what God has placed inside of me. Thanks always for loving me in spite of my imperfections and for always telling me that my stories sound good and are believable.

Thanks to my mother, Evangelist Carolyn Riddick, my sisters, Melina Mitchell and Marina Santos, for your support of me and because of this I have given birth to something great. Thank you to my godmother, Antoinette Milligan-Barnes, who rocks. She has been selling more of my books than I have, and I'm so grateful that she believes in me and loves me like her own.

Elissa Gabrielle, thank you for the encouragement and support on putting me out there with the interviews you have blessed me with and the road map on how to be a successful "authorpreneur."

Brenda Foster Love, for providing me with encouragement and literary nuggets in pushing me through the process of staying focused and completing the work.

Joylynn Ross, thank you for being the best editor ever. I'm extremely grateful to be a part of Urban Christian books.

Big thanks go out to Michelle Chavis and Tonya Bullock who work hard at getting me the publicity I need to take my dreams to the next level.

Bestselling Author Renee Flagler, thank you for just being you. I'm grateful to you for taking the time out to share with me the tools that helped get you to where you are now.

Thank you to everyone who purchases *Up Pops the Devil*. I appreciate you more than you know. A writer has no need to write if no one is reading. I hope each person who reads this book will be blessed and encouraged. Please tell all of your friends about it.

Thanks to all of my favorite authors, seasoned and new, who encourage me to keep my passion for writing alive.

Thanks to Jahzara Bradley, Carla Nix, Kisha Green, Dedrea Day & Chyna Blue, and Ella Curry of *Black Pearls* magazine, *Woman's Essence* magazine, Vanessa Richardson of *The Certain Ones* magazine, 21 Black Street, and many others for providing me the platform by hosting me as a guest on your radio shows or for featuring me and/or allowing me to write in your magazine as a platform to share my testimony and showcase my work.

And last but certainly not least, a big shout-out of thanksgiving to my earthly daddy, Gervasio Santos. You, my love, were always my biggest cheerleader and supporter. You pushed me when I didn't want to be pushed, and your love transcended the miles between us. RIP~love always, your baby girl.

Love and Blessings,

Lachá Mitchell-Scott

Chapter 1

"No, there has to be some sort of mistake," Serena screamed through the phone as her legs buckled and she fell to her knees.

"Serena, I'm so sorry. Unfortunately, there is no mistake, and we will schedule something within the next few days for you," the caller responded.

Nathaniel didn't miss the alarm in Serena's voice. He stopped dusting the entertainment center and turned his attention toward her.

Serena didn't wait for a response, but instead, she clicked the cordless phone off and lay on the floor in a fetal position.

"Hey, babe, who was that, and what did they say that's got you so upset?" Nathaniel walked over to where Serena was lying in the middle of the floor with a blank look on her face. Fancy, their three-year-old Shih Tzu, ran behind him nipping at his ankles.

"I'm sick of all of this." Serena rolled over onto her back and stared right through Nathaniel.

Nathaniel nudged her. "Slide over, baby. I want to lie down beside you," he said trying to distract Serena from whatever was said on the phone. Stress caused his eyebrows to arch and his forehead to crease with wrinkles. Not wanting to press, Nathaniel lay there and waited quietly for her to say something. He watched as sweat beads formed on Serena's nose and she rolled over onto her side. "Serena, baby, if you don't tell me what's going on, then I can't help you," he said staring at her intently trying to read her mind.

"That was Dr. Sinclair on the phone. Do you remember the tests I had done a few days ago?" Serena inhaled deeply before releasing the breath. "Well, the results are back, and the cancer came back with them," she said in disbelief.

"Aw, baby, I'm sorry. I thought that this thing was done and over with, but I guess God has other plans for you. What's the plan? Is there one?" In spite of the way he was feeling, Nathaniel's attempts to be strong for Serena were most important to him.

"I don't think that I can do this again, Nathaniel. I've been strong, and I've kept the faith, but the struggle is real," she fumed. "When I was diagnosed with throat cancer almost two years ago and God brought me through it, I didn't expect to have to go through that trial again. I don't understand why He allowed it to come back. Surely God has the last say-so in everything. Now, with the aggressiveness of its comeback, I'm just not as hopeful as I was the first time around," Serena said.

"Come to daddy." Nathaniel blinked back his tears and smiled. He lent a hand to Serena and gently pulled her upright before guiding her down onto his lap.

"Nathaniel, come on. I'm not in the mood to play. I'm serious about feeling like giving up," she whined, allowing herself to be vulnerable.

"I'm not making light of the situation, but I won't allow you to slump into some sort of depression." Nathaniel scratched his chin and silently questioned why God was allowing them to have to fight her cancer reoccurrence.

"Honey, I feel as if my life is spinning out of control. I've been in remission for over a year and nothing . . . Now look!" she screamed hysterically.

"Sweetie, calm down. We have to believe that God will show up just like He did the last time. Serena, please look at me." Nathaniel lifted Serena's chin so that he could look into her eyes.

Serena snatched her face from his hands, stood up, and walked away. She couldn't think straight nor have that conversation. Her emotions rode high like tidal waves, and then crashed, causing her to want to lash out. She ran to the bathroom, slammed the door, and began to scream and cry out, trying to rid herself of the fullness she felt in the pit of her stomach.

Wiping the tears from her eyes angrily, Serena admired the double sinks in the master bathroom. She loved the his and hers embroidered towels, washcloths, and a picture framed in gold with their initials inside. She had chosen the layout of the bathroom that was about the size of a bedroom. Running her fingers alongside of the double sinks, Serena reminisced on the excitement she and Nathaniel experienced when putting the specifications together for their home. The plush carpet comforted her bare feet, and she dug her toes in to feel grounded.

Fear of losing everything struck Serena, causing her to shriek and double over. In her mind, she fast-forwarded to dying before being able to bear any children. Images of baby showers and the first steps of a son or daughter flashed before her eyes. Whose initials would replace hers on the towels? Who would come in and remove every trace of her as if she'd never existed? The what-ifs and the who was driving her insane.

Fueled by a surge of frustration, Serena beat her fists on the wall and cried out, "Why, God, why are you allowing the devil to keep testing me? I don't think I'll make it this time. God, no . . ." Serena caved in to the pressure building in her chest as she caught a glimpse of herself in the mirror. She put her hands in her hair and shoved them through her short Afro and in the midst of an emotional meltdown, Serena snatched the pictures off of the wall.

She ran her fingers over the engraved letters that spelled out her name and Nathaniel's. Over and over she did that, kissing her pointer finger and placing it on Nathaniel's name. She recalled their wedding day as they opened up one of the 200 gifts they'd received. Smiling through her tears, Serena remembered when Evangelist Curry thrust her gift in Serena's face, practically begging her to open her gift. When Nathaniel and Serena ripped the paper from the smooth brown oak plaque that exquisitely beheld their names, everyone oohed and aahed over the gift.

While that day was a day of great joy and great anticipation for them both, the plaque reminded her that those dreams would no longer be a possibility. Enraged, Serena snatched the present from the wall. "Grr . . . This is so unfairrrr! Why do I have to give up my life? Why must I be the one sacrificed? God, why meee?" Serena yelled out in misery. The sounds of breaking mirrors and soap dishes could be heard crashing into the walls.

"Serena, open the door!" Nathaniel hollered twisting the knob only to find himself locked out of the bathroom. He banged and banged. "Serena?" Nathaniel was losing patience, yet he took a deep breath and tried again.

"Go away! I need to be alone right now. Please, baby, just go," Serena shouted.

"I'm not going anywhere. You're in there tearing up, and I'll be the one who has to clean it up. Come on out here so that we can talk about what's going on. Should I call Mom?" Nathaniel asked dejectedly.

"Call my mother? Why would you bring her into this? Can't I claim temporary insanity without you calling my mother on me?" Serena kicked the door, hurting her foot. "Ouch!" she howled.

"What is it? Did you hurt yourself?" Nathaniel's emotions ricocheted off of the bathroom door. He wanted to take the door off of the hinges to get in there to protect her, but he thought better than trying to force his way in. "Serena, please open the door," Nathaniel pleaded. "I didn't mean it to sound as if I was telling her on you. I only meant to imply that I'm sure that she would like to know about the diagnosis and be here to support you through this." His body went limp as he slid down the wall and sat by the door. Material things could be replaced; however, Serena couldn't be.

His heart ached as he listened to her cry out to God. He wished that he could hold her and comfort her, but he would respect her wishes and leave her be. The ringing phone got Nathaniel's attention as well as Fancy's. "Serena, baby, I'm going to see who's on the phone, and then I will come back to check on you." When she didn't respond, Nathaniel ran to get the phone, which was in the bedroom, before the voice mail picked up. Once again, Fancy ran beside Nathaniel barking.

"Hello, you've reached the Jackson residence. Who would you like to speak to?"

"Hey, man, it's James. You got a cold or something?" James was the administrator at Nathaniel's recreation center for at-risk youth and a good friend.

Nathaniel cleared his throat before resuming the conversation. "Oh, hey, bro, what's up?"

"I should be asking you what's up. You don't sound like yourself. Did something happen between the time you left here and arrived home? Is everything okay?" James interrogated him.

"Man, I don't know, to be honest. Serena just received some bad news from the doctor, and she's over here wilding out. To say the least, I feel my woman's pain, so if I sound a little off, that's the reason why." Nathaniel leaned against the oak dresser in the bedroom.

"Bro, I'm sorry about that. Do you need to do anything because I'm here for whatever you need? I've got you covered down here at the recreation center, and the kids will be fine," James said.

"Brother, I need for you to pray for us because I can already see that trouble's ahead. It was one thing when Serena had to cut her ministry schedule to just doing local engagements due to the treatments she needed. But even after she was given the green light and was free and clear of cancer, she refused to take any of the destination-speaking requests she's received." Nathaniel exhaled.

"I don't know if this news is going to further damage her self-esteem." Nathaniel walked to the bathroom, holding the cordless phone to his ear trying to listen to what could be going on with Serena.

"What do you mean you don't know what you're going to do? Bro, you're going to continue to trust God and hold on, my man. Maybe we can all go out and have a nice time. You know, dinner or something since it's been awhile since we've gotten together," James said.

"I'll check with Serena and get back with you," Nathaniel replied.

"Well, you think about it because there's no pressure here." James digressed not wanting to come off as being pushy.

"Nah, man, I mean . . . Yeah, I'll have to let you know when I can get Serena out of the bathroom where's she's locked up. I need to go and check on her now to make sure that's she's okay," Nathaniel said worried.

"Did Chris Shaw make it today?" Nathaniel gave James his undivided attention as he wondered where Chris could be. He'd been coming to the recreation center for almost a year, and at times he seemed to want to overcome his obstacles, but his absence made Nathaniel wonder what new had happened in his life.

"No, but I can check with Morgan and Tony, two of the center's kids, to see if they've seen him after I get off of the phone with you. I'll update you when I know something," James promised.

"I hope he's okay. You know he's had it hard with the bullying at school. I don't want anything bad to happen to him." Nathaniel knew that Chris wasn't mentally stable because all of the abuse he'd endured. His life seemed to go from bad to worse when he was placed into foster care after his father was found murdered behind some abandoned buildings near the railroad tracks. Depression had taken over his life, and he was the poster child of a whipping boy.

"Okay, you go and take care of your business and let me handle what's going on here. I love you, man," James said.

"Thanks, bro. Be good and let me know when you find out anything about Chris. I'll be on the lookout for an update on him," Nathaniel replied.

"Will do, my man. Peace out." James bid his brother farewell.

"Peace." Nathaniel clicked the phone off and dropped it on the bed. Jogging back to the bathroom with Fancy on his heels, he put his ear to the door and listened for any sounds. When he didn't hear anything it frightened him. "Serena, baby, are you all right? Please unlock the door and let me in." Nathaniel tried turning the doorknob, and surprisingly, this time it opened easily. When he entered and looked around the once-luxurious bathroom, tears came to his eyes. There was shattered glass everywhere. It looked as if a tornado had blasted through the room. Initially, he didn't see Serena so he walked into the bathroom, not realizing that she was balled up in the tub watching him.

"Nathaniel, I'm over here." Serena beckoned him over to her.

"Baby, are you okay?" Nathaniel walked through the crushed glass and swept her up into his arms.

Serena was spent and had calmed down considerably. Her tears resumed, soaking Nathaniel's T-shirt. "Babe, I'm really sorry for tearing up the bathroom. I just couldn't help myself. The mirrors seemed to be everywhere, and all I saw was my reflection of thinning hair, frail body, the past bouts of nausea and sickness. I don't want you to have to be on standby and watch me deteriorate before your eyes." Serena wept.

Nathaniel held his wife and cradled her in his arms. "Have I let you down yet?" he asked.

Looking up in his eyes for the first time she noticed how concerned he looked. "No, you've been there like you promised, and I can't help but to ask God why He gave you to me. I am not ready to discuss this with my family yet. Can you promise me that you won't go calling my mom or anyone else? Once I've had a chance to come to grips with the news, I promise that I will tell them. I'm sure that no one will take the news well, especially my mom and Amina." Serena looked away from Nathaniel as tears welled up in her eyes once again.

"There's something I've always wanted to know, and now I need to know." Serena braced herself hoping that Nathaniel wouldn't be upset. Silence enveloped the two of them; their feelings were on edge not knowing what direction the conversation was going to take. Serena usually felt at ease when she was with Nathaniel, but she was feeling unsure at that moment.

"Babe, what is it that you want to know?" Nathaniel asked, bringing Serena back to the conversation.

"Well, I don't want you to get upset, but I've always wondered if you married me because you couldn't live without me . . . or because I was sick? Did you feel the need to step up to be here for me because you felt guilty of not being able to do anything for your mother when she was sick?"

Nathaniel was caught off guard by the question, but he had pondered the same thing the day they were married ten months ago. He prayed long and hard before walking down the aisle to become one with Serena. He knew that he loved her, and he believed that he wanted to spend the rest of his life with her. However, he also wondered if his motives for marrying her were 100 percent because of his feelings for her, or was it to make up for having to stand by and watch his mother suffer from breast cancer.

Serena and Nathaniel hadn't been able to have date nights consistently the months leading up to her illness because of her various ministry assignments. When the diagnosis of her illness came, Nathaniel's emotions were on twenty, and unmerited guilt rode his back like a professional bull rider. No matter how he tried to free himself of the heavy spirit that weighed him down, he couldn't escape the images etched in the creases of his mind of his mother as she battled her illness all those years ago.

Serena could feel Nathaniel's heartbeat gallop like a horse running away from its tormenter as a tear fell on her forehead. She feared the worst. "Oh my goodness!" Serena snatched herself away from Nathaniel, becoming hysterical all over again. "You only married me because you felt sorry for me. You wanted to get with me, yeah, right. I knew that the whole thing was moving too fast." Serena paced the floor, shaking her head. "I asked you if you were sure. I asked you, and you lied to me repeatedly. I can't believe you . . ." Serena cried, acting as if her marriage was over as well as her life.

Nathaniel got up slowly, not knowing what to say. His emotions were all over the place knowing that he wasn't able to give Serena peace of mind. He knew that she was waiting for him to answer, but he didn't really have an answer for her at that time. Nathaniel's truth was that he knew that he couldn't live without Serena, but he also knew that her summation of his motives weren't 100 percent false.

"You don't have anything to say for yourself, do you?" she yelled. "Well, I have one thing to say to you, and that is, I didn't get here by myself. God healed me, or so I thought, but you never should marry anyone out of sympathy. I married you, mister, because you bamboozled me into believing that you wanted to be with me regardless of my illness. I gave you the easy way out many times—but no—you stayed because you were looking for some self-fulfillment." Serena walked up on Nathaniel and poked him in his midsection although she aimed for his chest. She was considerably shorter than he was.

"You treated me like a charity case, as if I needed to be rescued by you so that you could look up toward heaven and say, 'See, Mom, I did it. I helped someone, even though I couldn't help you.'" Turning away, Serena walked briskly into the kitchen with Nathaniel on her heels. She ranted and raved as she moved around the kitchen, seemingly looking for something else to destroy.

Nathaniel knew that he needed to try to diffuse the situation before things got way out of hand. He finally got the courage to walk in her direction, but she held her hand up for him not to approach her. "Serena, you're acting irrational, and you're upset, so I'd like to think you are speaking more from emotion than the person you know me to be." He attempted to walk toward her again, and she held up her hand to stop him again.

"Don't you even think about coming near me! I asked you what I thought would be a simple question, and I almost stopped myself, because I wasn't sure if I really wanted to know the answer. Knowing the truth, and then not knowing is something that has kept me on pins and needles. Man, don't you get it that I gave up all that I was to become right for you? In the beginning, your complaint was that I was too independent, so I fell back as to not be in competition with you. I allowed myself to love you after all the hell I've been through in my past." Serena slid past Nathaniel and almost ran back through the house to the living room and flopped down on the chaise lounge. "Fancy, stop that barking!" Serena chastised the pup as she nipped at Serena's ankles.

"Get away from me, Nathaniel. Maybe I really don't know who you are." Serena threw her hands in the air and stomped off down the hall to their bedroom and slammed the door.

Nathaniel rubbed his hands over his bald head and sighed. It was times like that he wished he had someone to talk to who wasn't expecting anything from him. His cell phone vibrated through his pants pocket, and at first he didn't answer it. He was sure that he knew who it was as he finally dug down into his pocket and retrieved the phone, which vibrated three times, and then stopped.

He looked at the screen and saw the name Malik, confirming that he was correct. It was really Melissa Wright, a member of Abiding Savior, who he'd dated a couple of times before getting with Serena. She'd been calling constantly the last two weeks, and although Nathaniel had ignored her calls before, he had become curious about what she wanted. The first time he called her, he'd promised himself that would be the last time he'd called. However, one call turned into two, and so on. Regrets of being in contact with Melissa tinged Nathaniel's heart and mind, but before he knew it, he'd added her number into his phone under an alias.

Instead of ignoring Melissa, knowing that Serena was upset with him, Nathaniel snatched his keys off the key rack in the foyer. He quickly ran out of the house and hopped into his car before he could change his mind. Locking himself in the car, Nathaniel pulled out his cell phone and called Melissa back. Mentally, he berated himself for leaving his wife alone. Despite how distraught she was, Nathaniel thought it would be good to get lost for a while.

"Nathaniel, how are you, honey?" Melissa answered on the first ring.

"I'm on my way over," he said and clicked his cell phone off before pulling out of his driveway. He didn't realize that Serena was watching him out of their bedroom window.

Chapter 2

Melissa Wright stood five feet three. She had long silky hair that was naturally bouncy. She looked like she could have modeled for *Vogue*, and she stayed on top of her game. Fresh manicures, pedicures, and Melissa's hair was always on fleek. For those that knew Melissa, they knew that she liked the finer things in life. She operated and owned her own hair/nail spa called "The Wright Touch." Looking in the mirror, she primped and checked her teeth to make sure no food particles were trapped in between them.

Laughing to herself, Melissa didn't believe for one minute that the marriage between Nathaniel and Serena would last. That's why she didn't raise an eyebrow when it was announced in church on that fateful Sunday that they were to be wed. Even his dramatic proposal and pathetic pledge of undying love and affection hadn't moved Melissa. She was biding her time until she could snatch him away from Mrs. Thing.

After months of calling Nathaniel with little to no success, Melissa believed that God was finally leaning in her direction. Just recently, Nathaniel had been calling her, and although she had to admit she was shocked at first, she bounced back quickly. He didn't say much when he did call, just friendly calls, probably to test the waters. Melissa didn't care about that; it was the fact that he called not just once, but a few times that had her mind swirling. She was determined to maximize every moment of his time that night. She would do whatever it took to cater to his every need—even if that meant that Nathaniel ended up going home to Serena later.

Scurrying through her house, Melissa spiffed up, making sure that there were no dirty dishes in the sink and that the bathroom was tidy. Sprinting through the house and back into the kitchen, she checked to see if she had some sparkling grape juice and some mango-flavored Moscato in the refrigerator. She wanted to be ready for whatever, but didn't want to come across as being too aggressive and turn Nathaniel off. Running to the master bedroom, she ran her finger up and down the body oils and body sprays she had lined up on her dresser, and decided on her favorite scent of them all, which was Moonlight Path from Bath and Body Works.

Melissa sprayed a good portion of her newest bottle on before tossing it back onto her busy dresser. She inhaled the scent, happy with her choice as the soothing fragrance tickled her nose. Looking into the mirror, she fluffed her hair, making sure that her locks looked neat. "Hmm, I need to make a trip the mall to get some more Moonlight Path and White Musk before the week is out," she said out loud as she took inventory of her stash. Needing to remain busy until Nathaniel's arrival would help Melissa to remain confident.

Rushing into the living room, she snatched her lighter off of the end table. She ran around the perimeter of the room lighting candles and Dream Spirit incense. Then she stood back and scoped the room in its fullness, making sure she hadn't forgotten anything.

Exhaling, Melissa smiled at the manifestation of her hard work. Throughout the years, she'd built her brand, and the Wright Touch had grown by leaps and bounds. The success of her business afforded her the 5,000 foot home that boasted four bedrooms. She used one of the bedrooms as a home office. It had three bathrooms, a large kitchen, and dining room. She even had a movie room, pool outside, a two-car garage that housed a candy-apple red 2015 Lamborghini, and her 2008 black Ford Mustang.

Checking her mental list of things to accomplish, she had done it all except for being married and having two kids. She figured that the dog and the picket fence could come later. Melissa sat down on the couch and wondered why she couldn't get a man. It really wasn't that she couldn't get a man, but the problem was that the man she wanted didn't want her, and he was married. She believed that if she joined the church and was nice to everyone that God would send her someone to take care of her and love her unconditionally.

"Nathaniel's finally coming over, and I won't allow this opportunity go to waste," Melissa declared to herself. She heard a car pull into the driveway and assumed it would be Nathaniel. She stood up and twirled herself around to fan out the fragrance she wore. The incense did its job by having the living room smelling right. A light haze filtered throughout the room. Melissa danced in little circles on her shag carpet. "He's here, he's here!" she squealed in delight. Melissa didn't want to seem desperate, so she let him ring the bell three times before sashaying over to the door, twisting the light switch on the wall to dim the lights, and let Nathaniel in.

Melissa widened the door . . . and time stopped for her. The smell of the Perry Ellis cologne Nathaniel wore wafted through her nostrils, causing her to feel woozy from the mixed smells mingling in the atmosphere. She held on to the doorknob as she struggled to regain her composure. Absently, she moved to the right to allow Nathaniel to pass by her. She even dismissed his rude behavior when he brushed past her without as much as a hello.

Nathaniel interrupted her thoughts. "Earth to Melissa, are you just going to stand there with the door wide open, or are you going to come over here and talk to me?" He had made himself at home on her tan leather couch and familiarized himself with his surroundings. When he and Melissa had dated, he hadn't gone into her home because he didn't want to give her the wrong impression. Even though that was the case, he still hadn't figured out what he was doing there and what he wanted to happen that night.

"Oh, I'm coming," Melissa said, closing the door, but not before taking a quick look up and down her street wondering if Nathaniel had been followed. "I guess I'm just having a hard time believing that you're really here. I felt like we left things unfinished when you decided to marry Serena not long after you told me you couldn't see me anymore."

Turning to face Nathaniel, she continued. "You hurt me, and you used me as a pawn in order to get to Serena." She approached him and stood there with her hands on her hips and began to rant. "I was good enough for you to wine, dine, and be your eye candy out in public. However, I wasn't good enough for you to put a claim on or a ring on this." Melissa thrust her hand into Nathaniel's direction, wiggling her ring finger for emphasis. She'd thought she would be okay with him coming over. That she could let bygones be bygones, but the rampage she was on exposed her heart.

"What are you going on and on about? I told you after a few dates where I was at with us. I'll admit that I tried cutting myself off from Serena, but I couldn't shake her. My going out with you was to free my mind of her and to be nice to you. You're a beautiful woman who has a lot going for you, but I had to cut you off in order to go hard for Serena. Plus, there were other things going on that needed my attention," Nathaniel explained.

Melissa took two deep breaths before continuing, "Well, is that why you finally started calling me? And now you're here, telling me how you really feel." Melissa began to cry.

"Melissa, look, I'm not here for that. I just got out of one argument, and I don't have the energy for another," he said, dismissing her tears.

"Well, did you really think that we would be buddy-buddy after what you put me through? I haven't seen you in over a year aside of seeing your backside at church while I watched you walk away with your precious Serena." Melissa's emotions ran over. She needed a drink.

"What's the deal with the candles and the incense?" Nathaniel asked, changing the subject.

"I don't know. I wanted to create some kind of ambiance in order to remind you of what we shared, but I'm messing it all up with my tantrums. I even had some sparkling grape juice chilling and a bottle of our favorite Moscato depending on how things went," she whined.

"Let me apologize to you for the way things went down. I used you for my own selfish desires. I wanted Serena to stop playing games with me, and when you came along, you showed me interest, and then one thing led to the next. I loved the time we spent together, but she always had my heart. I went for the next best thing, and that was you. We had a great time, but I think you're overexaggerating how things were." Nathaniel moved to sit beside Melissa on the couch feeling the need to touch her in order to make her understand where he was coming from.

"Oh my God, man, would you *listen* to yourself?" Melissa cried, popping up from the spot where she'd been sitting. "You're telling me that you plotted to use me just because you were sure that once Serena heard that you were seeing me that she would come running to you? I can't believe you, and you'd better not come near me."

Melissa moved out of Nathaniel's reach and headed into her kitchen. She opened the cabinet and took out a glass and slammed the door.

Nathaniel popped up just as quickly and walked behind Melissa into the kitchen. Standing with his hands in the air, he said, "Melissa, I know that it all sounds bad, and I'm sorry for hurting you. For me, we just shared a few dates, nothing more. How did I know that you would fall for me that fast? Needless to say, that's the reason I'm here." Nathaniel rubbed his smooth bald head, knowing that he was really there to get back into Melissa's good graces. He needed someone to talk to, and despite what didn't happen between them, he felt comfortable with her. He ignored the Holy Spirit when it urged him to go home before things went too far.

Nathaniel could hear Melissa's sniffles as he remained fixed in place, standing across from her. He felt bad for making her cry, and the tug in his heart coaxed him into getting close to her. When she didn't resist, he leaned over and wiped her tears away with his thumb.

Melissa regained the fire she had felt moments earlier and moved away from his touch. She turned to the refrigerator and pushed the jug of sparkling grape juice out of her way in order to reach the bottle of Moscato. Pulling it out, she filled up her flute with the drink. "You know you've got some nerve coming to my house with your tail tucked between your legs after all of this time." She turned the glass up to her mouth and gulped the wine down without so much as a blink of her eyes. "What do you want from me?" she cried, refilling the glass and repeating the process.

"I should be asking you what it is that *you* want. You've been blowing my phone up from the time I got married, and I've recently been responding. When we talk, you're just shooting the breeze, but I'm here now, so what are *you* going to do?" Nathaniel took Melissa's glass of Moscato and took a sip before handing it back to her. "It's rude not to offer your company something to drink. Can you forgive me for hurting you?"

"Nathaniel, why are you here? What's going on with you and Serena?" Melissa searched his eyes for answers, but found none. She pressed on. "Surely something is amiss for you to leave Miss Serena and wind up on my doorstep tonight."

"Melissa, can I have a hug?" Nathaniel knew he should have been at home getting the attention from Serena, but he also knew that would be impossible because she was hurting, and he failed at being strong for her.

Instead of answering Nathaniel, Melissa turned her glass up to her lips and gulped down the rest of her drink. "I usually only have one glass a night to wind down, but I'm going to need the whole bottle tonight." She turned to fill up the wineglass for the third time and against her better judgment, threw her head back and tossed the contents in the glass down her throat. She coughed due to the wine going down the wrong way.

"Lord, Melissa, is this the effect I still have on you?" Nathaniel laughed for the first time that evening. "Here, let me help you," he offered.

"No, don't come near me. I've called your phone like a hopeless romantic, wishing that you would answer and come running back to me. I've had dreams of you and me making love and becoming one with no Serena to compete with. She's living my dream, Nathaniel—*mine*. You didn't have to do things to make me notice you." Melissa stomped her bare feet on the hardwood floor.

"When you enter into a room there's an unspoken presence that precedes your entrance. My breath still gets caught in my throat when you walk into the church on Sunday mornings. Butterflies cause me to clutch my stomach when I think about the possibility of seeing you, and now here you are." Melissa had filled her glass for the fourth time and swirled the bubbly elixir around in her glass.

Nathaniel watched her drink glass after glass of the fruity drink. He didn't try to dissuade her, but he didn't indulge her either. His conscience was kicking his butt, but he tried his best to ignore the sirens going off in his head . . . and his loins. "I need to go. I shouldn't have come." Nathaniel decided to break out before he did something that he wouldn't be able to take back.

"What's the deal, Nathaniel? Serena not making you as happy as you thought she would? Did she go and get all high and mighty when God healed her from the cancer?" Melissa slurred her words as the tainted drink took its toll on her.

"Don't ever mention my *wife*. When I came here I was upset. I wanted to apologize to you, and I needed a breath of fresh air. Now, I'm thinking that it wasn't such a good idea after all." Nathaniel looked at Melissa with her wavy hair swinging past her shoulders. She was wearing all-black sheer material. He felt his resolve rapidly weakening. There was no denying the fact that he was still very much attracted to Melissa, but he couldn't admit that to her.

"I'm sorry to imply anything negative about Serena. I'm just a sore loser, and I have spent countless hours trying to figure out how I could possibly win you over. I do believe that you could have just called me to apologize. You can't get mad at a girl for hoping for more since you're here." Melissa smiled and placed the empty flute on the marble countertop. She began walking over to Nathaniel, but she stumbled. She would have fallen, but Nathaniel hurried to her rescue.

Caught up in the moment Nathaniel gazed into Melissa's glassy eyes, and he held her a little too long. When he looked at her, all he could see was Serena the day she almost fell and he was there to catch her. He closed his eyes with his thoughts still on Serena as Melissa pulled his neck down to meet her lips. She wasn't sure if Nathaniel was going to let it happen, but Melissa took her chances and kissed him. She watched him intently, but his eyes remained closed as he returned the kiss.

After the kiss ended, Nathaniel opened his eyes and looked at Melissa who had tears in her eyes. He knew that while she thought the kiss was about her, it wasn't. He knew that he was treading on dangerous ground, and the recent activity confirmed it. One more look in her eyes, and he fully gave into the moment. He captured her lips in his and held her tightly as he kissed her deeply.

Nathaniel wanted to erase the hurt that he caused Melissa, and she allowed him to go as far as he wanted. She didn't want him to stop; she let the moment play out. Knowing it was wrong, Melissa felt some sort of sick victory thinking that if Nathaniel came after her once, and then again, there was a great chance that she would end up the winner of his heart after all. That was what her mind told her, but her heart was preparing to lose once again.

"Nathaniel, are you sure that this is what you want?" she asked as they broke their kiss. Her body was craving his. All he had to do was say the word. Her inebriated state didn't help matters at all. She had an itch that only Nathaniel Jackson could scratch.

"Let's just live in the moment, shall we?" He waited for her response, but instead, she led the way to her bedroom.

***

"Where did he go? I can't believe that he just walked out on me like that. I'm not even sure how I should take that. And who was he calling on the phone before he pulled out of the driveway? He looked upset, but it's unlike him to stay away from home this long. I don't know if I should call my mother, but I need to talk to someone before I lose my mind with worry," Serena vented to the empty house. She picked up the cordless phone from the bedroom and dialed Nathaniel's cell phone. It went straight to his voice mail.

"You've reached Nathaniel Jackson. Your call is important to me. I'm sorry that I can't take your call at this time, but if you leave a detailed message, I will call you back at my earliest convenience." A beeping sound pierced her eardrum.

Serena couldn't begin to understand what was going on in her life. Tired of crying and feeling sorry for herself for the time being, she ran into the bathroom, forgetting the mess she'd made earlier. "Ouch!" she screamed out as she hopped on fragments of broken glass. She cried out in pain and cursed Nathaniel for not cleaning up the mess before he left and herself for not using the bathroom in her bedroom.

She winced in despair as she teetered on her heels as fast as she could to the kitchen. In tears, Serena retrieved the first aid kit in the cabinet above her head. When she looked down she saw all of the blood that dripped from the open wounds on the bottoms of her feet. She was glad that she had suggested linoleum floors because she would have to clean the traces of blood she tracked through the house as well.

Serena knew that Nathaniel wouldn't be happy about the floors being bloodstained because he took so much pride in their home. During the planning phase of the five-bedroom, three-bathroom home with pool room/

man cave that Nathaniel had his heart set on, he'd taken his time in going over the blueprints with the builder and upgrading the appliances to give the house a more chic look.

Serena sat on the floor and unpacked the first aid kit. "Gauze, Band-Aids, alcohol wipes, and Neosporin. Lord, I'm so tired. If someone would have told me years ago that this would be my lot in life, I would have laughed in their faces. I had big dreams that didn't include me being stricken with a cancer so aggressive that I'm afraid to live day by day. I've never been a scared person before, but I have a new respect for anyone paralyzed by the fear of what their reality is." Serena spoke into the atmosphere having grown bored of the mundane quiet that threatened to choke her out.

Looking at the traces of blood on the floor, she thought about the loss of dreams, loss of passion to be, and the possible loss of life. Her mind raced with thoughts from the day she was in church on that fateful Sunday, giving God praise and worshipping her King. She'd been victorious over cancer, and her first Sunday back to church was a memorable one. The next few moments, hours, days that turned into the next year of her life were terrifying to have to relive. She couldn't escape the nightmare she'd endured even while awake. Serena was absorbed in her thoughts, and she didn't hear Nathaniel come into the house.

He saw specks of blood and followed the trail that led him into the kitchen where he found Serena looking spaced out. "Baby, what did you do?" Nathaniel cried out. He felt responsible for the scene before him. He almost slipped in wet blood as he ran to his wife, calling out to her and still getting no response. It wasn't until he reached down and shook Serena's shoulder that he was able to get through to her.

Serena snapped back to the present, and when she looked up at her husband, tears were running down her face. The anger she felt toward him for leaving her evaporated as relief took over now that he'd returned. Nathaniel scooped her up and lifted her to carry her to their bedroom.

"I had forgotten about the mess I'd made earlier and ran barefoot into the bathroom. I hope that there isn't any glass still in my feet. I'm sorry. I don't know what came over me earlier. Can you forgive me for blowing up at you and questioning your motives for marrying me?" Serena asked.

Nathaniel stood by silently, allowing his guilt to consume him. He never should have left her alone. A good husband would have remained by his wife's side no matter what was going on. His heart was being torn apart while he watched as Serena cried out to God, pleading with Him to cancel the illness that placed her life at risk again.

The fear of losing Serena made Nathaniel weak enough to run to another woman. He sat motionless as he watched the scenes play out before him. He was tearing down everything that he'd prayed for. His wife didn't need him giving her doubts of his love and commitment to her and their marriage. But what had transpired between Melissa and him couldn't be erased.

"Serena, you don't owe me any apologies. I understand that your emotions are all over the place. I'm the only one who should be saying I'm sorry. I feel like an idiot for running out on you, but one thing I know is that I love you with everything in me. To answer your question, I wanted to marry you because I love you and want to be able to take care of you as sort of a redemption-type thing because I couldn't help my mother when she was ill.

"I've never felt sorry for you, Serena." Nathaniel carried her to their bedroom. "Sit still while I tend to your wounds, and then I'll clean the bathroom." Nathaniel's shoulders sagged as he felt himself becoming the man that he'd promised he'd never be if Serena ever became his wife. He'd had such high hopes that he wouldn't allow the pressures of life cause him to run away and seek comfort in the arms of another woman.

Chapter 3

The doorbell rang and Crystal Sampson hurried to answer the door. Her hips swished to and fro as she moved quickly through the living room to receive her expected guest. She threw the door opened and stepped to the side. "Hey, come on in." Crystal's eyes said that she approved of Tremaine's crisp cool white shirt, white cap, and stonewashed jeans.

"Don't you look lovely?" Tremaine stepped forward, and then took a half step back and checked Crystal out from head to toe. His eyes drank in her smooth face with the twinkle in her eyes and smile playing about her mouth. He gulped before speaking. "I tell you, I feel like the luckiest man on earth. These are for you, my lady." Tremaine pulled a bouquet of flowers from behind his back and bowed in front of Crystal, flashing all thirty-two sparkling white teeth of his.

"Tremaine, we don't operate believing in four-leaf clovers and luck. We are people of faith." Crystal walked away. As if Tremaine and the flowers were an afterthought she looked over her shoulder and said, "Thanks for the flowers; they're beautiful. Can you close the door and bring those in here to the kitchen?"

"I'd be happy to. What's that smelling good?" Tremaine followed Crystal like a lovesick puppy. He was enamored with her beauty and was overjoyed about how their relationship had progressed over the last year. Things had really gone full-speed ahead after Crystal's son, Jonathan's, troubles and her daughter, Serena's, illness had seen its best days.

"Tremaine, do you mind putting those flowers in a vase for me? I'm almost finished cooking dinner, and we will be able to eat soon." Crystal stirred the sweet potatoes, and then moved on to the next pot which contained fresh collard greens, ham hocks, onions, and other spices. "Would you like something to drink? There is a variety of juices and teas in the refrigerator. You know where everything is. You aren't a visitor anymore." His heart leaped as she acknowledged that she and Tremaine had been dating for a year and things were getting pretty serious.

Tremaine put the flowers in a large vase and took them onto the screened-in porch. The rays of sun followed his trek through the house providing warmth along his way. Spring was his favorite season of the year as new birth was sure to take place. He couldn't wait until the threat of snow and ice was just a distant memory. Tremaine thought back over the year that he and Crystal had been seeing each other. He smiled at the possibility of spending the rest of his life with her. The transition in his life was a positive one, with him rededicating his life to the Lord. He'd even begun working every other weekend in order for him to attend church, and he was now singing in the choir.

It didn't take long for Crystal to lay on the guilt by pressuring him about having his work schedule changed to nights on Sundays. She loved throwing shade his way with slick comments from time to time about not being "visible enough" in the ministry. Tremaine shook his head as he had a conversation in his mind about what he would say the next time Crystal brought up the subject. He was prepared to lay down his law. Deep in thought, Tremaine vaguely heard Crystal's voice calling out to him.

He could hear her more clearly as she walked out to find him on the porch.

"Tremaine, is everything all right? I got worried when you didn't come back to the kitchen," she said to his back side.

"Um, yes, all is well." His hand was beginning to cramp, and it dawned on him that he'd never set the flowers down near the window. Feeling as if he'd been caught with his hand in the cookie jar after being told not to get any, Tremaine set the vase in a corner where the sun could hit the flowers.

Instead of leaving Tremaine to himself again, Crystal waited until he turned to face her. There was a faraway look in his eyes that caused her stomach to quiver inside. She wasn't sure what it was about, but wisdom . . . or fear kept her from addressing it. She reached out and touched his arm.

"Sweetie, come with me. I've already set the table, and I hope that you're hungry. If I say so myself, I declare that I put my foot in this dinner today." She talked fast, praying in her spirit for a shift in the somber mood that seemed to have swooped down upon them. Moving out of the way, she allowed Tremaine to lead the way. She knew that sometimes she could be pushy, controlling even. Sitting at the dinner table, Tremaine's once-dry mouth had begun to water. Finding his voice, he looked at Crystal and stretched his hands out to hold hers. She followed his gesture, and he prayed over the meal. They said "Amen" in unison.

"What did you think of the service today?" Crystal asked as she dug her fork into the homemade stuffing she'd prepared from scratch.

"Service was good today. I tell you, those youth are something else. All that energy they have makes me wanna join the mime team. I wouldn't even mind putting that white gooey stuff on my face; it looks awesome on the kids. I tell you, Crystal, those kids are serious about the Lord. You can tell they are doing more than just going through the motions." Tremaine picked up his turkey leg and took his first bite. "Mm, this is good, lady. I tell you, I now know what I've been missing all these years."

Crystal looked like she could bust a gut looking at Tremaine and seeing him smile. She kicked her feet together under the table and acted as if she had never prepared a meal for him before. She loved cooking for her man. He always complimented her on her delicious array of baked dishes with parmesan and savory spices. "I'm glad that you like it," she said blushing.

"On a serious note, those babies just blessed my soul this morning. I'm so happy that we have good leaders in place. I tell you, I don't know what I'd do without Sister Felisha. I knew that she'd be perfect for the youth ministry. I've watched how she has grown by leaps and bounds, and she is such a good mother to her own children. I'm so glad that God doesn't look at our past and disqualify us from working in His Kingdom. I've watched Him use the kids within the ministry to build her self-confidence. Although she had a rough start, God knows that her latter days shall be way better than where she come from." Crystal wanted to say something else, but she decided to hold her peace.

Tremaine listened with his spirit and felt a tug on the inside. The more Crystal talked, he meditated on how good God had been to him. Although she was speaking about Sister Felisha and how rough she had it, Tremaine revisited the heartbreak he endured with his first wife, Riva.

When he found out about her infidelity, he confronted her about it. He loved her more than life itself and wanted to work it out, even though she had betrayed their marriage vows. He had every intention on forgiving her and moving on with life. When the rumors started, Tremaine didn't want to believe them, but when a close friend confirmed the rumor, he had no choice but to check out the story.

One night instead of reporting to work, Tremaine called in sick because he hadn't been able to reach Riva at work. Each time he called her desk phone it went straight to voice mail. It wasn't like her to not answer her phone or at least return his calls. He remembered leaving about twenty messages that day. Each time he called, his nerves ran amuck. He knew that he had to find out for himself if his wife was stepping out on him with his best friend, Jamani.

Tremaine waited until dusk and drove over to Jamani's house. Instead of pulling into the driveway, he parked down the street where he had a clear view. It didn't take long for Jamani to come down the street, followed by Riva who pulled into his driveway behind him and exited the car. Not able to contain his anger any longer, Tremaine left his car on the street and ran to Jamani's house. He pounded on the door until someone opened it, and when the door swung open, Jamani and Riva both stood there with shock on their faces. He remembered that day like it was yesterday; it was the day that Tremaine confronted his worst fear outside of dying.

Tremaine just stood there and cried because he didn't have the energy to fight. He remembered asking Riva to come home so that they could talk about what was going on, but acted as if Jamani had evaporated into thin air. She refused to come home and told him that she was leaving him. Riva never even apologized for hurting him. She looked as if she could finally exhale and live her life the way she wanted to.

Days later, Jamani called Tremaine and even went to the home he and Riva once shared. However, Tremaine hid behind the door of his home with the bottles of alcohol that helped him deal with his miserable state. Days turned into weeks, weeks into months, and months into years, and Riva never returned to the home to get her belongings. When Tremaine got the strength to part with her for good, he called Goodwill to come pick up her things. He had them all packed and lined up on the front porch and down the sides of the driveway like trash. The doorbell rang but Tremaine never went to the door. He was passed out drunk with tears dried on his face.

"Tremaine, what's wrong? Why are you crying?" Crystal had watched him leave her mentally, and she wanted to know where he was and what had him so upset. A wave of nausea caused her head to swoon. She blinked and took a deep breath to settle her stomach. Tremaine didn't answer, but it was clear to her that he was hurting. Alarmed, Crystal rushed from her chair to reach out to him.

Suddenly, the doorbell rang, startling both Crystal and Tremaine. "Honey, why don't you go into the bathroom and clean yourself up. I'll go and see who's at the door." Crystal didn't move until Tremaine got up and went to the bathroom down the hallway. She stayed glued in place, still wondering what had just taken place. She needed to ask Tremaine more questions. She was certain that would be the only way to really get to know him. Up until now, he had been guarded, but she felt a shift taking place and the dam breaking to his being transparent.

Crystal finally came back to herself and went to answer the door. Upon seeing her granddaughter, Amina, along with her fiancé, James, standing at the door she cringed. One side of her mouth was raised up, and the other seemed paralyzed, not moving at all. She couldn't find her voice.

"Hey, Gran-Gran," Amina said cheerfully leaning over to give her grandmother a big kiss on her cheek. But when Crystal didn't say anything in return she wondered if it were a bad time. Looking back at James, he shrugged his shoulders, feeling as if they were intruding on something.

Slowly Crystal was able to make her mouth obey, and she pushed the words from her mouth. "Hey, baby, what brings you by?" she asked in a strained voice.

"Gran, we could smell the fragrance of your cooking all the way across town. I figured that you had prepared a big meal. You know you prepare meals for folks the size of an army. James and I were about to head to Golden Corral, but I suggested that we come here instead. Is that okay?" Amina asked, trying to read her grandmother's expression.

James tried to save his fiancée by speaking up. "Hey, Pastor, we can always come back another time." He stepped in front of Amina. "I tried to tell Amina we shouldn't just pop up without letting you know beforehand." His expression looked grim. He was still trying to learn the hard woman. Amina nudged him from behind, almost knocking him into Crystal.

"Amina, that's not ladylike. I would like to think that was a one-time thing. You shouldn't ever put your hands on your man unless you are giving a back rub, foot rub, or hugging him." Crystal set her granddaughter straight quickly. "Come on in this house. You know I have nosey neighbors," she snapped. "I don't know what's gotten into you young folks these days. When your grandfather was alive, I would never think of raising my hand to him." Shaking her head, she left James and Amina standing there with stunned looks masking their faces.

James didn't think that it was that serious, but apparently to Crystal it was. He followed her into the house, but he turned around when he didn't feel Amina behind him. Looking back, he saw that she was still standing out on the porch. "Amina, come on before your grandmother comes back out here," he prodded.

Amina rolled her eyes, not moving. She stood outside feeling unwelcomed, pouting with her arms crossed above her chest.

"Don't worry about it. I know you were just playing," he whispered.

They heard Tremaine's silky voice in the background, and then looked at each other, knowing that they had interrupted something between the two. "Who's was at the door, baby?" Tremaine asked when Crystal returned to the table. He sat back down at the table to finish eating his meal although his appetite had taken a hiatus.

"Amina and James, but I don't know why they haven't gotten in here yet. Amina?" Crystal called out from the dining room. Getting no immediate response she hollered through the house without getting up. "James, are you all still holding my door open?" she asked.

"Um, no, ma'am, I mean, yes, ma'am, we're coming now." he hollered back from the porch. Turning to Amina, she still refused to move until she figured out who that woman was and what that surly lady had done with her grandmother. "Amina, come on, baby. It's going to be okay. Let's just go inside, have dinner, and get out of their hair. It's obvious that we came at a bad time. I can feel the tension in the air. Next time, will you listen to me and call first?" James stressed, not really wanting to stay but not knowing how to get out of it at that point.

If looks could kill, James would have turned into a pillar of salt by the hardness that mingled in Amina's eyes. He walked over to her and pulled her into the house, closing the door behind them. He then escorted her into the kitchen, silently praying that by the time they reached the dining room that Amina would have shaken the chip off of both her shoulders. "Hey! Brother Tremaine! How are you feeling, my man?" James said with exaggerated happiness in order to break the cloud hovering above.

"Hey, man, I'm blessed. How are you?" Tremaine stood up and received a manly hug from James. He looked over James's shoulder and smiled at Amina. He could see that something was wrong, but when she caught his eye, the hard lines around her face softened and a smile covered her face.

Amina felt the tightness in her chest dissipate. She could see the pain in Tremaine's face and the redness of his eyes told the story behind her grandmother's terse words. Deciding not to take her grandmother's outburst personal, she relaxed as she looked over at the enormous spread of food. "Gran, you've outdone yourself. Did you know that James and I would show up here famished after that awesome service today at church?" Amina picked up the bottle of hand sanitizer that sat on the edge of the table and squirted the liquid into her hands, and then gave James some before setting it back down.

James wasn't sure what to think as his eyes darted from side to side and back again. Turning toward Amina, he struggled to figure out what was going on with her. She was acting if the last ten minutes didn't happen, but he'd let it slide for the moment. Deep in thought, James rubbed his hands together methodically. He replayed the scene in his mind from the time they got out of the car. Admitting to himself that he was uncomfortable with being there, James had lost his appetite.

"James, where are you?" Amina had reached over to still his hands that he was still rubbing together although they were as dry as a board. She had snapped him out of his daydream, and he gave her his full, undivided attention. "Are you going to eat today, or will you just be watching everyone else eat?" She scolded him as if he were a child.

Embarrassed, James stuttered, "I-I was just thinking about something, but I'm not that hungry right now," he said, leaning back in his chair.

"What do you mean you're not hungry? *You're* the reason we're here, *remember?* We left church, and everywhere we passed, there were lines wrapped around the buildings as people waited to get in restaurants. You were complaining about having stomach pains, and when I suggested Wendy's, you hollered something about not wanting fast food on a Sunday. That's when I suggested that we come here because I knew that Gran-Gran had cooked up a storm of food." Amina looked at James as if she couldn't believe the flip in his attitude. "What did you do, just turn your stomach off?" She shook her head and grabbed a plate from the center of the table.

"Amina, mind your manners. The young man said he wasn't hungry right now, so why are you beating him over the head with what was?" Crystal was in disbelief. She started to wonder how the day started out so nice and peaceful—to end up with attitudes flying high and everyone speaking to one another as if they hadn't just left church.

"Weren't you listening this morning to the sermon about avoiding strife?" Crystal asked, reminding them of the message she'd preached from the morning's service. "I tell you the truth, y'all are bickering over nothing at all. Your fruitless conversation is as worthless as those bad checks that members write and place in the collection plate on Sunday morning." Crystal laughed to herself, but when she looked around the table at the sullen faces she realized that she was laughing by herself.

"So how are things going with you two lovebirds?" Tremaine asked, hoping to break the iciness that surrounded them. His eyes had cleared up, and he felt stronger. Picking up his glass of iced tea he swirled the half-melted ice pieces around in the glass before taking a swig of the watered-down drink.

Amina ignored Crystal and turned her full attention toward Tremaine. "I thought we were fine, but now I'm not so sure. I mean . . . We were fine before coming here." Amina rolled her eyes toward her grandmother and smacked her lips.

Crystal cut her eyes at Amina. Determined not to give anymore place to the devil, Crystal barreled ahead, trying to shift the uneasiness by changing the subject altogether. "Have you spoken with Serena?" She directed her attention at Amina.

Although Amina was fuming inside, she had to admit even if to herself that she was embarrassed by the way she responded to James. She shuffled her food around on her plate with her fork and kept her head bowed, not really wanting to look up to answer her grandmother. "I haven't spoken with her since last week," she mumbled, hoping that the next question would be directed to someone else at the table. "I called her, but only got the voice mail. When church let out today, she and Nathaniel left, barely acknowledging us, so I'm sure something is going on, but not sure what."

"Chile, I can barely hear you. Can you open up your mouth and enunciate properly? You know the way you were just doing as you were going in on James here?" Crystal pointed her fork in James's direction.

Amina placed her fork down into the still-full plate of colorful food and looked her grandmother square in the eyes and exhaled. "Gran, it's obvious that we came at a bad time. I don't know what was going on here before James and I got here, but whatever it was has surely affected you negatively. I can't remember the last time you raised your voice at me. Now that spirit of anger has transferred over to me, and you're reprimanding me for that too. Maybe we should go." Amina stood abruptly causing her chair to screech against the hardwood floors that Crystal saved up for years to have put in.

James couldn't understand why Amina was taking things so personally. She had stated the obvious, yet she retaliated as if she had no self-control. He carefully stood and pushed his chair back. "I'm sorry about all of this," he said, throwing his hands up in the air in despair.

Tremaine cleared his throat and spoke. "Crystal, isn't there something that you want to say to your grand-daughter? I don't know how this afternoon has turned into an avalanche of attitudes and strife. I must confess that Pastor and I were having a conversation, and it really hit home with me and my past. I believe that's when things got funky. She still isn't sure why I reacted the way I did, and you all showed up before I had the opportunity to explain to her why," Tremaine explained.

"You don't owe anyone an explanation about anything," Crystal snapped. *I can't wait until they leave so you can explain this to me.*

"Crystal, that's enough." The bass in Tremaine's voice made Crystal flinch. He knew the time would come that he would have to set some boundaries if they were going to continue to move forward in their relationship. He had been praying that Crystal wouldn't feel the need to be domineering about everything now that he was in her life, but unfortunately, she still felt the need to be in control.

James prepared to leave. He was ready to go and wished that they hadn't dropped by. Amina watched the two men grab each other for a brotherly hug, but she didn't hang around to bid anyone farewell. Confusion blanketed her face and heaviness settled in her gut. She dared not call on the Lord in that moment because she knew that there was no way that God would recognize her. She left James inside and stomped to the car, got in, and slammed the door.

"How could he just throw me under the bus like that?" Amina asked herself. She shuddered as she rewound the previous events. She didn't remember ever having an encounter with her grandmother that had her so flustered. Amina calmed down the longer she sat in silence. Twenty minutes later she saw James walking toward the car with two plates in his hands, smiling.

"Babe, what's going on with you today?" he asked, slinking into the driver's seat of the car. "Can you hold these plates? Your grandmother wrapped up our food since we didn't finish eating. You know, I think that all of the tension was just a big misunderstanding. Surely you don't think that Pastor Crystal meant to upset you, do you? I mean, it's clear that something deep was going on that affected everyone's mood." James struggled to get his seat belt on.

"Did you see how she talked to me? And why did you throw me under the bus? You knew good and well that I didn't mean any harm when I nudged you. I still can't believe that I lost control like that. I understand what you mean now by not showing up anyplace unannounced." Amina crossed her arms and stared out of the window.

"Babe, I'm totally surprised at the way you acted today. I mean, why did you allow your grandmother to provoke you like that? Is there something going on between the two of you that I don't know about?" James hadn't started the car, but turned to face Amina.

"I didn't mean to get so offensive, but something in me just snapped. I don't want for her to think that I *put my hands on you!*" Amina slammed her hands on the dashboard of the car.

"I'm still in shock about the whole thing. I know I disrespected her, and for that I'm wrong, but we've never interacted that way before. Did she think she was talking to Auntie Serena?" Tears trickled down Amina's face.

James was stunned. He knew that he should have tried to comfort Amina, but he didn't move. Caught off guard by her explosive display of emotions, he stayed still. His mind was on overload with thoughts of what he needed to do, but he didn't do any of them. His face donned a dumbfounded look as he sat there until he was sure that Amina was through venting. Silently, he cranked the car and slowly backed out of the driveway. A blaring car horn caused them to jump, and James pressed the brakes so hard that the force caused them to lurch forward.

"Babe, are you all right?" James looked over at Amina with his heart pounding like he'd run five miles.

"Yeah, I believe so. I'm just a little shaken up." Amina held her hand to her chest thinking about how silly she'd behaved and how near they came to being in an accident. She opened her mouth to apologize for her attitude. "James, I acted a pure fool with my Gran today, and you know we could have been hit by that crazy driver, and I never would have been able to talk to Gran again." Amina looked to see if the car had at least stopped, but she saw no sign of it.

"Calm down, baby, we're okay." James jumped out of the car and ran around to Amina's side of the car to comfort her. He snatched the door open and picked her up out of the car. "Shh, baby, it's okay. Please don't talk like that. I would never be able to forgive myself if anything happened to you while you're in my care, and it would devastate me if any harm came to you in my absence. I love you, and I can't wait to be able to call you my wife." James wiped the tears from Amina's eyes and kissed her gently on her lips.

Holding her tightly in his arms he whispered, "Forever, my lady . . ." and rocked her back and forth in his arms until he felt her heartbeat slow down and continued to whisper sweet nothings in her ear until she began to laugh.

"Break it up, you two," Jonathan teased. He had Ariane park on the side of the road after seeing the driveway blocked with James's car and the collision that almost occurred. After being convicted of drinking and driving, Jonathan's license had been revoked, and he was going faithfully to alcohol anonymous as well as seeing his probation officer twice a month.

"Hey, Daddy, how are you?" Amina squealed like a little girl. Her tears were replaced with joy at seeing Jonathan. She broke the embrace James held her in and jumped into her father's arms. "Daddy, I missed seeing you at church today," she said.

"I'm good, thanks to Ariane." He smiled at Ariane as she approached the trio. Letting Amina go, he reached out for Ariane's hand. "I know, baby, I actually went to church this morning with Ariane," Jonathan gazed at Ariane beaming proudly. He had yet to share some things with her about his past, but he was enjoying the friendship they shared. Jonathan knew that she wanted more, but he wasn't sure if he could commit to being anything but a good friend to her.

"Hi, it's good to see you both again," Ariane spoke to Amina, slightly turning to include James in the salutation.

"How are you, James?" Ariane reached out her free hand to shake James's hand.

Amina and James smiled at Ariane. Feeling more like herself Amina joked, "Oh, you know Gran is going to pitch a fit when she hears that you went to another church. She's really big on the family worshipping together. So what brings you guys by?" Amina asked, prepared to warn them about possibly rethinking going into the den of wrath that she'd barely escaped from.

"Your father thought it would be a good idea to come over and see Pastor Sampson for a while before I drop him back off at his apartment," Ariane answered.

A chill ran up and down Jonathan's arms and back. Every time he thought about going back to his lonely apartment, depression crept in. He was used to living in his plush apartment up in Manhattan. Jonathan had lost almost everything when he nearly killed himself and another innocent person when he wrecked his car.

Jonathan couldn't outrun the demons of his past nor the pain he'd endured when the love of his life had broken up with him and left him alone to raise their child. His life took a turn for the worst when he engaged in a homosexual relationship. Jonathan spent years running from his past, and when he'd finally returned home just recently, his mistakes followed him there too. It didn't help that he had also picked up drinking alcohol in excess. When his sentence was initially passed down he'd agreed that it was reasonable. He would accept anything to keep from having to spend another night in jail. Jonathan paid restitution and would be on probation for the next four years.

Once Jonathan had moved out of Crystal's house, he'd missed her nagging him about this or that. Before anyone else could say anything, Crystal appeared at the front door and hollered out to her family standing around holding council, "Hey, no one invited me to the party." She placed her hands on her hips and waited to be acknowledged by her family.

"Mom, we were just coming in to see you." Jonathan waved good-bye to Amina and James. Grabbing Ariane's hand, he proceeded up the steps and stopped at the door. "Hey, Mom, how are you?" He leaned over to kiss Crystal's cheek.

Ariane moved around Jonathan to hug Crystal. "Hi, Pastor Sampson, you're looking beautiful this afternoon." Ariane envisioned herself in the turquoise one-piece linen jumpsuit.

"Where did you get that from? I think I'll get one for myself." Ariane made small talk with Crystal as Jonathan slid past them and went into the house.

"This old thing? I just pulled it out of my closet and threw it on. But if you're serious about getting one, then you can check online at Ashley Stewart's. I only paid twelve dollars for it. It's comfortable, and well, ya know . . ." Crystal smiled and closed the door. She sashayed into the living room where she could hear Tremaine and Jonathan laughing.

Ariane laughed at Crystal as she sashayed in front of her and followed Crystal into the living room to sit down beside Jonathan.

"Hey, Ariane, how are things at work?" Tremaine asked while flipping channels on the flat-screened television set.

"You know how it is at the hospital. There is an influx of patients, overworked doctors, and being a nurse like myself, we are the unsung heroes and who are also underpaid," Ariane explained. "Those are the two main reasons that the turnover rate is so high, and we are constantly understaffed. I'm so glad that I love working with people, and I'm not just there for a paycheck," she explained.

"Yes, you're right about that," Crystal replied. "The part about having a heart for the people, it's the most important aspect of our jobs. I had been alone for so many years that my only interaction with other people was when I would go to work or go out to the grocery store."

"My patients are my family." Tremaine couldn't get another word out before he heard Crystal grunt behind him. He turned to her and smiled before turning his attention back toward Ariane.

"Mom, can I talk to you for a moment in the kitchen?" Jonathan broke in, hoping to deter something from jumping off because when those two got together, they could talk for hours nonstop. He lifted his mother under her elbow and steered her into the kitchen to have some one-on-one time with her.

"Jonathan, that was rude of you. How do you know I didn't want to sit in and hear the rest of what Ariane was saying?" Crystal snatched her arm out of his grip and huffed.

"Mom, the only thing I could see about to happen was that you were getting ready to get turned up over nothing." Jonathan laughed at himself.

"Why are you here? I've had a rough afternoon, and I don't need anyone else putting a damper on my Sunday afternoon." Crystal didn't mean to snap an attitude at Jonathan, but he had taken her away from what she felt like was a very important conversation. Her thoughts had reverted back to what Tremaine had said at the dinner table. She wanted to pay attention to her son, but her heart was in the other room testifying that his only family were the people he pushed around in wheelchairs and transported from floor to floor.

"Mom, hello, where were you just now?" Jonathan slapped his hands on his legs.

"Jonathan, why are you yelling at me? You know I don't play that!" Crystal couldn't bring herself to admit that her stomach was trembling inside, wondering if Tremaine would remain in her life or not. Refusing to be anything less than Tremaine's first priority, Crystal had checked out of the conversation with her son and had gone deaf as fear rushed to her head clogging her eardrums.

Chapter 4

Serena woke up that morning wishing that she could sleep in. But the aroma of fresh coffee beans danced in her nostrils, giving her a boost of energy. Rolling over, she knew that she wouldn't be able to go back to sleep even if she wanted to. Sitting up and preparing to stand, Serena landed flat-footed on the floor and howled. "Ow! Ouch, ouch . . ." She teetered on the backs of her heels.

Nathaniel heard the commotion that came from the rear of the house. Abandoning the eggs he was frying, he ran at lightning speed to check on Serena. "Babe, what's wrong?" Wearing a mask of terror, Nathaniel reached out to break Serena's fall as she fell to the side of the bed, nearly missing it.

"My feet are still a little tender, and I hollered more from the fear of hurting them than the actual pain. The coffee was calling me, and I got too excited, I suppose." Momentarily forgetting what had transpired the week before, Serena held onto Nathaniel, enjoying his fresh scent. "I love you, Nathaniel Jackson, and I love being Mrs. Serena Jackson."

"You sit down." Nathaniel guided Serena back down onto the bed. "I'll be right back. I believe your eggs are burning right now. Your coffee is on the nightstand; help yourself," he said over his shoulder.

Serena fixed her pillows up behind her head before preparing some coffee. She smiled as she looked at the drink tray that held everything on it that she loved in her coffee. "He knows me so well." She chuckled.

After dumping the caramel into her monogrammed mug, which bore her initials, Serena stirred the contents and pulled the cup to her lips to take her first sip of the drink. She smiled and nodded her head in approval. Closing her eyes, she relished the cup of homemade caramel macchiato and wondered where Nathaniel got the recipe from. He didn't like using the Internet much because he wasn't savvy in typing, but he had definitely blessed her taste buds early that morning.

Nathaniel returned to see Serena's face with her eyes closed, yet her lips were pursed as if savoring the coffee blend. He carried the food tray closer to her, hoping that the aroma from the food would awaken her senses and that he'd be able to pull the mug from her face. Still feeling guilty about seeing Melissa, Nathaniel was probably going overboard, but he didn't care. His wife looked to be at peace, and that's all he wanted for her.

Fancy ran into the room, obviously hungry from smelling the bacon, eggs, toast, and fruit that Nathaniel had prepared for Serena. "Babe, open your eyes because your meal is being served," he said with a wide-toothed grin spread across his face. He moved the tray in front of Serena's nostrils and awaited her reaction.

"Mmm, this smells delish. You've outdone yourself, Mr. Jackson. Now why don't you sit down with me and help me eat all of this food? You know I can't handle all of this in one sitting, and we can't afford to allow it go to waste," she said.

"I'd rather hold you in my arms, my lady." Nathaniel's deep voice dropped an octave lower. The dog barked and yelped, wanting to be picked up to get to the food. She ran around in tiny circles at Nathaniel's feet. "Fancy, go eat your food," he demanded, already tired of the dog's hyperbehavior. He gently moved Fancy by using his leg to push her backward to keep from stepping on her.

"I love the sound of that, Mr. Jackson, but this coffee though, where did you get the recipe? I know that you didn't go on the World Wide Web because you hate sitting down to a computer to do anything," Serena gushed with love.

"Well, you're right, but I had James go online to check out the recipe. You were the only one I would go through such great lengths to please." Nathaniel laid the charm on thick, adding, "Now can I get the hug I've been standing here waiting on since I came back into room?" Nathaniel poked his bottom lip out as he waited.

Serena placed the cup down on the table and stood, loving the height difference between Nathaniel and her. "I'd be honored to be able to hold you for any additional moments that we are afforded." She stepped into his embrace, closed her eyes, and held onto him as remnants of the news she'd received from the doctor stormed her mind. The thoughts weren't gentle in their return, but their reappearance was vigorous and forced her to remember all over again. Recurrent images of her situation ripped her peace to shreds. Where there was once amity there was now chaos and betrayal. Serena felt it in her spirit but as of yet, she just wasn't sure to what degree the treachery had reached.

Nathaniel's body reacted to Serena's closeness, but his transgressions wouldn't allow him to show her how badly he wanted her. He knew that if Serena were to ever find out about his tryst with Melissa that she would never look at him the same, and he wouldn't chance losing her, not that way.

Serena's emotions had her feeling out of sorts, and she may not have said much, but she felt Nathaniel's behavior change toward her. Fear struck in the pit of her stomach and resonated through the tips of her toes. She didn't want to let on that she perceived anything out of the ordinary. In spite of her troubled spirit, she looked up at her husband with tears in her eyes and kissed his lips. Nathaniel desperately wanted to make things right between them, despite the fact he'd crossed the line with Melissa. He leaned into the kiss, hoping that his shame would take a backseat so that he could connect with his wife.

Pulling away, Nathaniel said between sensual pecks across Serena's face and neck, "I love you, sweetie, and I don't ever want to live without you." His lips brushed against her bare skin, and his heartbeat galloped like a racing horse. Lines creased Serena's forehead, which represented the complexity of what was to come with her relationship and health as Nathaniel's fears presented his indiscretions of that night with Melissa that could be the result of him losing his wife. He tried unsuccessfully to block the images of Melissa's face from popping up in his mind. He rushed to undress his wife and became one with her. Knowing that there would be questions later, Nathaniel selfishly pressed his full weight upon Serena, forgetting how vulnerable and fragile she was.

"Ow, babe, you're hurting me," Serena cried out. She wasn't sure why Nathaniel was being so aggressive because that wasn't like him.

"Oh, I'm sorry. I didn't mean to hurt you." He apologized as condemnation was birthed out of desire to crucify and annihilate the deed he'd committed with Melissa. In the midst of what Nathaniel had hoped would be a great makeup session, he softened, losing his zeal. Serena felt her husband's body reject her and wondered if things would be that way indefinitely. She tried kissing him to recapture the passion he had displayed just moments ago; however, the mood was ruined.

"What was that about?" Serena asked staring into Nathaniel's eyes, searching for a sign, but found no consolation when he dropped his gaze from hers. Bewildered, she watched him untangle himself from her slender frame and retreat into the bathroom. He closed the door, and then she heard the lock click. Not considering her nakedness, Serena knelt beside her bed and entered into the throne room in prayer.

Nathaniel didn't have the courage to look at his reflection in the mirror. "What have I done? God, I need for you to help me. Please help me to come to terms with breaking promises to Serena and myself. I believed that my love for her was stronger than what I'd felt for any other woman. I broke my vows," he whispered in torment. Upon hearing her husband's cries, Serena was prompted to pray even harder. As she tried to figure out what to pray for, she vaguely heard the shower running. Feeling a burden in her spirit and trouble looming like storm clouds before a violent storm, Serena wailed. She groaned and grunted as if she were in the delivery room attempting to push a baby through the birth canal. The more Serena groaned, the more a vision flashed behind her closed eyelids . . . and she saw Nathaniel and Melissa.

The vision wasn't detailed, but there was no mistaking who the people were that God revealed to her. Up pops the devil. He was always on the prowl, but she wanted to believe that God would counterattack the fiery darts of the enemy on her behalf. She'd heed the warning and thanked God for showing her that danger lay ahead. Serena couldn't deny that this wasn't of the devil, but God.

She pulled herself up from the floor when she heard the shower stop and sat on the edge of their bed watching as Nathaniel emerged from the bathroom wrapped in a towel. An internal war raged inside of her as she thought of the vision God had showed her. The rumbling in her spirit birthed questions about his whereabouts that night he left. She never asked him, and he'd never offered an explanation. A burning sensation bubbled in Serena's gut as fiery darts assaulted her mind, body, and soul. Nathaniel seemed oblivious to her sitting there eyeballing him, accusing him before he'd even been charged with a crime.

The ringing phone interrupted Serena's thoughts, even though she didn't move to answer it. She thought that Nathaniel left the room to go answer it, but as she listened she heard the voice mail pick up. The greeting picked up, and then Serena heard Nathaniel's recorded voice speaking to the unknown caller, letting whoever it was know that they were unavailable at the time. The next sound she'd heard was the beep, and then she heard Amina's voice.

Serena sat unmoving and watched as Nathaniel came back into the room with a glass of tea. Quietly, he carefully put lotion on every part of his body and continued to get dressed as if he was the only person in the room. Serena believed that trouble was surely crouching at their door as she remembered the vision that she believed God had shown her. She was ready to unleash her arsenal of questions on Nathaniel; however, she decided to seek God instead. She didn't want to cause herself any undue stress because she had bigger fish to fry with her health.

She'd hoped that Nathaniel would accompany her to the doctor that afternoon, but the strange way he'd been acting caused her to rethink her decision on asking him. She knew that if he'd agree to go, she wouldn't be able to resist badgering him with questions that wouldn't get her anywhere near the truth of what was going on with him and what Melissa Wright had to do with it. She'd just have to go alone because having him in her presence would only bring forth trouble, and she was stressed out enough as it was.

Nathaniel was dressed and out the door before Serena could get her bearings. Fancy was running around yipping, and her little feet could be heard scratching on the floor as she ran through the house. He didn't bother saying anything to Serena when he left, which only heightened her fears all of the more so. She dared not move from the bed until she was sure that Nathaniel wouldn't be turning around to come back to the house. She didn't even have the strength to holler at Fancy for making all of that noise and acting crazy.

Serena finally washed her face, threw on one of her Nike jogging suits, and took Fancy out for her morning romp. To her surprise, when Serena opened the door, Crystal was standing on the other side.

"Mother, what brings you by?" Serena tightened her grip on Fancy's leash and headed out of the house.

"Well, good morning to you too, Serena. I came by just to check on you, that's all," Crystal said waiting for Serena to exit so that she could close the door.

"Oh, everything is just dandy, peaches and cream. I'm just taking Fancy out for her morning walk. Would you care to join us and get a little exercise?" Serena walked the dog over into the yard where lots of grass covered the ground and allowed her to handle her business. She figured that's why Fancy was running around acting as if she'd lost her mind . . . Or else she'd sensed something wasn't right in the home.

"Why haven't we heard from you? Nathaniel hasn't called, and you know we are a tightknit family. I get worried when I don't hear from either of you," Crystal said. She adjusted her velour pants and looked at Serena. "Look at me. Do you think that I came out here to get some exercise? I wish I would have come by a little later on since you're out here with your little pooch. I'm definitely not interested in perspiring in *this* suit," Crystal said twirling around to be seen.

"Well, Mom, either you can stay or you can go. You know that I've gotta tend to my li'l Fancy-Wancy," Serena said avoiding Crystal's glare because she didn't want her mother to think that anything was amiss. She removed the leash from Fancy's neck and let her roam the yard while she talked to Crystal.

Crystal watched Serena's body language and felt like her daughter was holding out something important, and she wasn't leaving until she got all the details. "Humph, where is my son-in-law? I thought I would see him this morning as well. Isn't he off on Thursdays?" Crystal probed, using her mental calculator to add things up. One, Serena was being evasive, and two, Nathaniel was usually home on Thursdays, but he wasn't today.

"Well, he's at work. Usually he's off, but he got dressed after making me a nice breakfast and left. So, I assume he's down at the recreation center. He's been talking to James about some little boy name Chris, who's been missing in action." Serena tried to recall some of the conversations that Nathaniel and James had in the last couple of weeks. She'd say whatever she could think of to stop Crystal's interrogation.

"Oh my, well, I hope that the child is found. I couldn't imagine if your brother or you had gone missing when you were little. I don't know how I would be able to handle the realization that someone would be so cruel as to take y'all or to not encourage you to come home," Crystal said in sincerity.

Serena watched as Fancy took off running toward the edge of the yard where safety was, and into the street where danger and death found her. A car came down the road blasting loud music. The driver could be seen ducking down as if he or she was in search of something.

Horrified, Serena screamed out, "Fancy, nooooo!" The next thing that could be heard was the driver of the car screeching to a halt, but not before rolling on top of poor little Fancy, and her dog collar getting caught someplace under the bumper of the car.

Serena cried as she ran toward the street, barely looking to make sure that no other traffic was coming toward her. "Oh my God," Serena cried hysterically grabbing her head. "Mommy, why are you just standing there?" she hollered over her shoulder.

The person driving the car jumped out. "Ma'am, I'm *so* sorry. I wasn't really paying attention to my speed. Please tell me what needs to happen now. My husband isn't going to be happy. Must we call the police? Isn't there some way that we can handle this without the law being involved?" the woman pleaded.

Serena's only concern was Fancy. She looked under the car and saw her baby lying unmoving on the ground with blood dripping from the corner of her mouth. "God, why?" Serena asked. "It's just too much. I can't take anything else." She felt like she was going to have a nervous breakdown.

"Baby, it doesn't look like we can do anything else for Fancy. By the looks of things, she's gone." Crystal was upset and didn't know how to comfort her daughter. "Serena, do you want me to call the police?" She'd heard what the lady said, but she didn't take orders from strangers. If Serena wanted the police involved, then so be it. Crystal pulled her cell phone out of her pants pocket.

The lady skittered over to Crystal and said, "Miss, are you calling the police? I mean, didn't you hear anything that I said? I can't afford to have the cops involved." She turned to Serena and asked, "Miss Serena, that's your name, right?" The woman's face was beet red as she stomped around, flailing her arms looking like a fish out of water. "Look, I'm really sorry about hitting your dog, but can we figure out something here that doesn't involve a call being placed to nine-one-one?" She twisted around to look at Crystal again.

"Serena, do you want me to call the police?" Crystal dismissed the cra-cra woman and directed her full attention to Serena, who sat rocking her lifeless dog. "Serena? I need to know what you want me to do." Crystal felt helpless as Serena continued rocking back and forth in the street. She worried as oncoming traffic was at a standstill. "Serena, baby, you've gotta get out of the street because those cars need to get by," Crystal cried hysterically as the car horns honked behind them. She didn't know what to do, so she dialed Nathaniel's cell phone.

"Jackson's Development for Youth Center, how can I direct?" James answered but was cut off in midsentence.

"James, is Nathaniel there with you?" Crystal asked in a panic as she watched the cars wrap around the corner.

"Pastor, is this you?" James asked unsure, hitting the button to place the phone on speaker.

"It's me, and I need to speak to Nathaniel nowww!!!" Crystal shouted over the blaring horns and the lunatic hollering in the background.

James heard all of the commotion on the other end of the phone and forgot to put Crystal on hold. He dropped the phone and ran to Nathaniel's office. He stopped when he saw one of the boys' mother with her head bent over and Nathaniel rubbed her back as if trying to console her. When the noise kept shooting from the phone that sat on the front desk, James sensed the urgency of what he needed to do. Rapping on the window lightly, he hoped to get Nathaniel's attention. When he saw Nathaniel look up, he curled his finger in a beckoning motion. Nathaniel held his hand up as to say hold up, which caused James to begin waving his arms furiously.

The look on James's face convinced Nathaniel that he was needed ASAP. He touched the woman's shoulder that sat in his office sobbing and advised her he would be right back before going out into the bay area to see what the emergency was.

"What's up, man? You know that Chris has been missing for over a week now, and Ms. Shaw is in there wilding out, as she should be." Nathaniel paused when he heard the muffled noise coming from the front desk phone. His eyes traveled to where the phone was lying. "What—who is that going ham?" Nathaniel asked.

"Look, man, I'm sorry to have to interrupt you in there. Pastor Sampson is on the phone, and she needs to speak with you. I don't know what's going on, but it sounds serious," James explained.

Nathaniel didn't know what to think. The sounds of sirens alarmed him more than anything as his thoughts went to Serena. He ran to the phone and snatched it up as fear ran through him.

"Pastor, is it Serena? What's going on, and where are you? Are those sirens I hear?" Nathaniel asked without so much as taking a breath.

"Nathaniel, Serena took Fancy outside so that she could handle her business. We got to talking, and I guess we took our attention off of the puppy for just a moment. The next thing we knew, Fancy had taken off into the street and was hit by a car. The driver of the car is here acting totally irrational, and Serena is still sitting in the street holding Fancy who's dead while cars are becoming backed up because they can't pass by on the street.

"I tried to get her to stand up and move out of the road in order that the woman who hit Fancy could move her car. However, it's like she doesn't even hear me talking to her. She's holding onto Fancy and rocking. I need for you to come right away because she said something about God doing this to her, and now He's taken her best friend." Crystal was at a loss for words.

"I'm on the way and thanks for letting me know what's going on. Serena's going through a lot right now. I just hope that she doesn't have a nervous breakdown," Nathaniel said.

"Why would she be having a nervous breakdown? Oh, never mind. I'll see you when you get here." Crystal clicked her cell phone off and went back over to where the police were trying to coax Serena up off of the ground. Watching the chaos that was going on, she kept her distance and did what she did best, and that was to pray.

Chapter 5

"Babe, I've got a surprise for you." Nathaniel came into the house and kicked the door shut behind him, carrying a box with a red bow on top.

"I'm in here," Serena replied. She'd been depressed and emotional ever since Fancy got killed two months ago. Once again, she'd shut Nathaniel out, and he'd taken the easy route by seeing Melissa more often than he should have.

"Peeuuuuuu, when are you getting up?" Nathaniel swiped at his nose as he approached the bed balancing the box in the crook of his arm.

"What's in the box?" Serena ignored the question. She tried to look excited, but she just wasn't feeling it. Depression over the loss of Fancy and her suspicions about where Nathaniel had been spending his time kept her from going to the doctor to get a treatment plan rolling. It was no secret that she was disgruntled at the realization that Nathaniel didn't seem to try very hard to be there for her. It was no secret that time was running out, but the fact alone did nothing to push Serena to do the things needed to sustain her health for as long as she could.

He tried to dismiss the staleness coming from the room and said, "Tadaaa!" Nathaniel put the box down on the floor and opened it, pulling out the cutest little pup. He smiled, holding the two-toned black and brown Chihuahua up against his cheek.

"Nathaniel, whyyyy did you go out and get another pet? I killed Fancy. What else has to die around here before you get it? I'm not fit to take care of anything or anyone, especially myself. You're adding insult to injury, but you can always take it back," she said.

"Oh, come on, Serena. You didn't kill Fancy. It was an accident. Things happen, and unfortunately, it happened on your watch." Nathaniel put the dog on their bed and waited to see if she would change her mind. He figured if he just gave them a few minutes alone that by the time he returned to the room, she'd be holding the pup and falling in love all over again.

"I'll just give you two a few minutes to bond. I'll come back in a little bit. I have a few things to handle in the living room." Nathaniel left the room as his cell phone vibrated in his jeans. He ignored the call, knowing that more than likely it was Melissa. He rushed to pick up everything and ran it into the laundry room as someone on the other side of the door impatiently pressed the doorbell over and over again.

Nathaniel didn't want anyone to know that he'd resorted to sleeping on the couch ever since Fancy's demise. Serena had been difficult to deal with since then. The first two weeks she didn't do anything but cry and walk the house at night. Even by week three he'd hoped that her stank attitude would be gone, yet she continuously pushed him away, shutting herself off from the world. Nathaniel had felt as if his hands were tied. He had to call in the family to be the support he would need in order to help Serena make it through the depression and her health issues.

"Hey, hey, come on in," Nathaniel cracked the door, looking over his shoulder to make sure that he hadn't left anything behind. Satisfied that he'd cleared away any signs of trouble between Serena and himself, he cautiously moved away from the door. Holding on to the doorknob, he allowed Crystal, Amina, and Tremaine into the house. He wiped the sweat from his brow and tried to prepare himself for talking to the family about Serena's health issues.

"Where's Serena?" Crystal asked as soon as she stepped into the house with Amina trailing her.

"Uncle Nathaniel, it's good seeing you. It's been a while," Amina said, kissing him on the cheek and heading into the formal living room. "Hmm, wonder what's going on here. I can feel it. Something isn't kosher," she mumbled to herself.

"Yep, my man, it's been a minute since I've seen you at Bible study." Tremaine followed by giving Nathaniel a swank handshake they had come up with.

"I know, there's just been a lot going on, and, well, I'm doing the best I can," Nathaniel said. The half-truth that he allowed to fall from his lips was getting easier and easier with each lie he told.

"Y'all come on in and sit down. Make yourselves comfortable and let me get straight to the point." Nathaniel followed them into the living room.

"Where's Auntie Serena?" Amina asked, concerned because of the uneasiness that lingered in the atmosphere. She'd felt the heaviness when she came in, and the only time she experienced that type of pull on her spirit was when something was going on. This was one of those times, and Amina hoped that they weren't having marital problems or anything that couldn't be restored.

"Well, that's the reason I have invited you all over today." Nathaniel rubbed his head. "Mom, the day you called me and asked me what Serena was rambling on about, she was feeling as if she'd lost her grip on reality. A couple of months ago, Serena went to have routine tests done to make sure that she still had a clean bill of health.

We were both confident that all was well since she'd had tests done before and everything was fine.

"Dr. Sinclair called a week later with some stunning news." Nathaniel took a breath before speaking again. Everyone's eyes were glued to his lips, and it felt as if time had stood still until he revealed what needed to be shared. "To make a long story short, the cancer is back. It's spread to her liver and bones. Serena made me promise that I wouldn't say anything about her diagnosis.

"Serena said that she would let you all know when she was ready. She's been having a hard time since then and doesn't know that I'm sharing this with you. It's been two months since then, and Serena still hasn't made a move to go in to meet with her medical team. They are supposed to be working together to come up with a plan to battle the cancer." He sighed and braced himself for the responses from the people who loved Serena as much as he did.

Crystal felt herself tense up and grabbed Tremaine's hand, squeezing it hard. She had so many questions, but didn't know where to begin. Opening her mouth to speak, Crystal's voice was void of words as tears trickled down her face. Tremaine rubbed her hand, hoping to console her, although he too was in a state of shock at the news.

"Where is Auntie? Why isn't she out here with us talking about this?" Amina didn't have anyone there to rub her shoulders or to encourage her through this. She pulled out her cell phone to call her father. While she waited for Jonathan to pick up the phone, she asked aloud, "Can someone tell me why my daddy wasn't included in this family meeting?"

"I'm sorry, Amina; he should be here as well. Of course, he's welcome to come on over if he can make it," Nathaniel assured her, wishing he'd thought to call him.

Amina left the room with her cell phone glued to the side of her face, bypassing Serena, who had finally emerged from her palace, her bedroom, with the pup in tow. The smile she wore fell from her face as she saw her family sitting around with looks of sadness on their faces. Serena wasn't sure what to say when she looked at her mother's tear-streaked face.

The realization of why her family was there looking like it was the end of the world infuriated her. She figured that Nathaniel told them about the cancer, even though she'd asked him not to, and anger burned inside of her.

"Family, what are you doing here?" Serena asked, looking around the room at the faces staring back at her, but no one said anything. She felt in her gut that she knew exactly why they were there.

"I invited them over to discuss my concerns about you and your health," Nathaniel came right out and admitted. He knew that he should have discussed it over with Serena before involving them in their personal affairs, but he felt that his hands were tied by her recent behavior.

"How dare you? Why would you call *my* family over here unbeknownst to me so that you can talk about me and my issues?" Serena put the dog down and walked over to Nathaniel and poked him in his chest.

"Serena, what's gotten into you?" Crystal finally found her voice and jumped up from the couch. Tremaine stood to grab Crystal's arm and guide her back down to the couch.

"It's all right, Mom," Nathaniel said to Crystal as he held Serena's arms down to her sides and pinned them there until her fury subsided. "I called them here because you've been locked up in our bedroom for weeks, Serena. I'm worried about you, yet you don't seem to care about anyone but yourself. Everything that happens to you happens to us."

Nathaniel turned Serena around to face her family's worried looks. Amina had returned and sat quietly as sadness surrounded them all. Deflated, Serena fell to the couch and dropped her head. She felt ashamed by her actions, and she'd let her peace be stolen away, along with her health and her husband too. She'd neglected her family and herself by indulging in a pity party that spanned for weeks with no visible end in sight. Her emotions would kidnap happiness, faith, and joy from time to time, so she'd resorted to sleeping and eating comfort foods.

"Auntie, I've missed you, and I believe it's safe to say that we all miss you." Amina took the silence lingering in the room as an open door to speak. "Even though you're still coming to church, you've changed. It's not like you to turn down ministry engagements, but now it all makes sense. The heaviness I felt when I came in is due to all that you've had to endure since the call from your doctor. I wish you would've just talked to us, or even just me," Amina cried.

"Look at you! Your hair is matted, your skin looks ashy, and you smell." Crystal jumped right in to scold Serena. "You've got the nerve to come in here and try to beat your husband up for caring about you since you didn't care enough about yourself to let us know what's going on. I'm surprised at you," Crystal yelled in anger. She wasn't as mad at Serena as she seemed; she was mad at the devil and how he'd popped up to rob Serena's health *again*.

"Nathaniel, how come you kept this from us for so long?" Tremaine asked as if he'd been out of the room during the earlier part of Nathaniel's conversation. "You know how hard this is on everyone."

"It was my hopes that Serena would have told you all by now. Once again, the only reason I called you all here is because Serena has alienated me. This intervention was necessary because she's been holed up in our bedroom for the last month or so. I figured that if Serena wouldn't communicate with me that she might listen to you all," Nathaniel sighed.

"Well, when are we going to find out what we can do about these results?" Crystal asked.

Everyone looked over in Serena's direction, but she was trying to look busy with the pup that she declared earlier she didn't want.

Serena ignored her family as if they weren't watching and waiting for an answer. She kneeled down to pet the dog, saying, "Tango is your name. Tango Jackson, gotta get you a dog collar with a name tag. Nathaniel brought me this as some sort of peace offering, ya know? Well, I accept your gift, but I'd also accept the truth." She looked up at him teary-eyed.

Serena stared into Nathaniel's eyes for so long that beads of sweat popped out on his bald head. Silence engulfed the room since no one knew what Serena was talking about. They saw how uneasy Nathaniel was at Serena's request of some truth, and their inquiring minds wanted to know as well. The doorbell rang again, and Amina went to answer the door expecting Jonathan to be on the other side. To her surprise, it was Jonathan and James, and she was glad to see them both. They exchanged hellos and followed Amina back into the living room.

"Good evening, everyone. I hope you don't mind, but since Ariane is working, I asked James to come by and pick me up. So, what's going on?" Jonathan inquired taking his hat off and sitting on the sectional that didn't look crowded.

"Hey, son, it's good to see you," Crystal said, happy that her son was looking like the pillar of health and still seemed to be sober.

"You're here, big brother, because someone thought that I needed an intervention and called in the Sampson Calvary. My cancer came back, and it's metastasized. It's spread to my liver, and although I received the news over a month ago, I've yet to go see the doctors to get a medical plan together so that I can be treated," Serena said matter-of-factly.

"Okay, then, let's settle this now." Jonathan leaned against the mantle of the fireplace. "We won't know what the odds are if you continue to delay going in to see what can be done to help you. Time's running out, and we need to know what we are up against."

"In order for us to know if we can beat this thing for good this time, you're going to need to call and get that scheduled, Serena." Crystal pleaded with her daughter who was still busying herself with the puppy. "We will be here for you, and we'll even go with you if you if you'd like. Please, let's call the doctor right now because I'm so afraid that I am going to lose you. None of us want to lose Serena, do we?" Crystal posed the question to the group.

"No," the group said in unison.

Chapter 6

Serena finally decided to go to meet with Dr. Sinclair, her oncologist, to see how bad the cancer really was. As she looked for something to wear, she pushed clothes back and forth on the closet racks. Her emotions were on twenty as she thought back to her reckless actions of wallowing in self-pity for nearly two months. Serena was positive that her lack of motivation to go in to get started on treatment was to her detriment.

She decided not to let anyone know that the appointment had been made. Her family was already worried about her, and Serena didn't want anyone to go with her because she felt the need to be alone for whatever news she would be given. It gave her some sense of peace. Whereas it seemed more logical to let her family know what was going on so that they could be there to support her, she wouldn't be able to bear seeing the hurt on their faces when she received the devastating news from Dr. Sinclair. Dr. Sinclair would be relieved to see her come in since she'd been calling Serena nonstop since the results came back. Fear and disappointment dictated Serena's lack of response when the doctor would call. She intentionally allowed Dr. Sinclair's calls go to her voice mail each time.

She jumped in the shower, flinching as the hot water hit her back. Exhaling, Serena lifted her head and stood directly under the wide showerhead. The hot water was supposed to rejuvenate her; however, it seemed to only drain her of any energy she'd mustered up to crawl out of bed and press forward. She was too tired to cry and too weak to scream for some type of release from her pent-up frustrations.

After Serena's shower, she walked into her bedroom to get dressed. Glancing at the clock, the red letters stated that the time was one fifteen p.m. She'd decided on crème slacks, a black sweater with hanging scarf, and her Michael Kors leopard print wedge boots. Serena turned around in front of her floor-length mirror. She'd made sure that her clothes weren't too roomy because she'd lost quite a few pounds in the last couple of months. Forcing herself to eat since the results came back was a chore, and recently she'd been nauseated at the smell of most cooked foods.

She applied her makeup, and then sprayed some Suave flexible control mousse into her hands and rubbed it evenly throughout her short hair before rushing out the door. Making sure that the door was locked behind her, Serena jiggled the knob on the door, and then walked briskly to the car. The sun was blinding, but it was still chilly enough to cause her to shiver. She popped the lock on the door with her keyless remote before tossing her purse onto the passenger's seat and getting in.

"I'm here to see Dr. Sinclair, please," Serena said to the receptionist upon check-in.

"Hi, your name is . . .?" the clerk asked.

"Serena Sampson and my birth date is February second, nineteen seventy."

"Ah, here you are," the clerk acknowledged as she looked over the page full of names. She used a yellow highlighter to cross Serena's name out on the form. "Please take these forms and fill them out to give to the nurse when she calls you."

Serena smiled at the clerk and took the papers along with a clipboard to her seat. Looking over the questionnaire, the questions were familiar to her. She hated having to fill out the paperwork knowing that the clinic already had her medical history on file. She'd checked the last question, which asked her about having any type of implants or hearing aids, when she heard her name being called.

Exhaling, Serena braced herself for the inevitable. She stood, nodded her head at the nurse, and followed her back to an examining room. Having had her weight taken, Serena looked at the scale sadly as the numbers reflected her weight as being fifteen pounds lighter than the last time she'd weighed in. Serena had to wait thirty minutes for Dr. Sinclair to come in to see her. There was a soft knock on the door. "Come in," Serena called out and mustered up a smile although her nerves were on edge.

"Prophetess Serena!" Dr. Sinclair squealed, happy to finally see her patient and friend.

"Hey, Doctor," Serena returned the greeting with mock excitement. She stood to give the physician a hug, and then moved to sit back down.

"So how have you been feeling, Prophetess?" Dr. Sinclair sat opposite Serena and laced her hands across her lap, looking intently at her.

"I've had better days, Doctor. I know that I should have come in a lot sooner, but just to find out that the cancer had returned has been devastating. I've been depressed ever since, and it didn't help that my li'l pal, Fancy, was hit by a car." Serena dropped her head.

"Well, I'm really glad that you came in today. I was worried that you wouldn't come back in. I can only imagine what you've been dealing with since we called with the test results." Dr. Sinclair shuffled the papers in the folder she was holding until she found the one she was looking for. "Let's get started. When you came in for testing two months ago, the findings from your computerized tomography scan, also known as your routine CT scan, showed where the cancer has returned and has penetrated other areas of your body." Dr. Sinclair handed the results to Serena to look at.

Reluctantly, Serena took the paper and perused the information on it. She recognized the term metastasis, which meant the spread of the cancer cells. Handing the paper back to Dr. Sinclair, Serena inhaled deeply through her nose and exhaled slowly with her head thrown back on the chair as tears ran into her hairline. "What does this mean for me? I know that I didn't help anything by waiting so long to come in."

"It means that first, I would like to get some blood from you, and then we can discuss treatment options. I've already let the nurse know what I need, so she will be right in. Do you have any questions written down that you would like to have answered?" Dr. Sinclair asked Serena sympathetically.

A weary look made its way to Serena's face. "No questions." She closed her eyes and tried not to focus on what was to come.

"Okay, well, she should be right in, and then I will come back in so that we can discuss where we should go from here."

Serena smiled at Dr. Sinclair and nodded her head as a wave of nausea hit her. Thinking it was her nerves she breathed in and blew the air out of her mouth slowly. There was no way that she could have prepared herself for what she'd find out.

Chapter 7

"Grrr, I'm sick of this!" Melissa shrieked. She threw her phone on the couch, upset that Nathaniel had bamboozled her heart again. She'd always been told that if she's fooled once, shame on them, but if she's fooled twice, shame on her. "I've been trying to call him to find out why he's been avoiding me all of a sudden." Melissa was back to watching his backside walk into church on Sunday mornings. He knew where she sat because she never switched her position at the end of the pew, regardless of how many times she'd been asked to move for different reasons by the ushers.

Melissa paced around, wondering why Nathaniel had begun to ignore her calls by sending them to voice mail and blocking her text messages. Her mind was made up that Nathaniel would speak to her and another day wouldn't go by before that happened. "Ha-ha-ha, we'll see who has the last laugh. Little Miss Serena thought that she'd won because he married her instead of me, but I've got news for Mr. Jackson, and he's gonna hear from me right after service today."

Melissa walked over to her dresser and picked up the pregnancy test that bore two red lines. "I'll be the one giving Nathaniel his first son or daughter, and there's no doubt in my mind that once Serena finds out, she'll send him packing."

Feeling giddy like a schoolgirl who had her first crush, Melissa pranced over to her floor-length mirror and dropped her robe to the floor. She admired her sexiness as she rubbed her hands over her smooth skin, settling on her flat stomach. "I'm gonna have a baby, I'm gonna have a babe," Melissa guffawed out loud and ran to get in the shower before she was late for church.

By the time Melissa arrived at church the praise team at Abiding was amped. When she got to her pew, she noticed that Trina Clark, her best friend since beauty college, was sitting stretched across the pew, taking up more space than needed. "Girl, move over. I know you see me standing here," Melissa said moving at lightning speed into the pew and almost sitting on Trina's Bible bag and tambourine.

"Well, just disrespect my things, would you?" Trina snapped, moving her things over in a huff. "You know you should have gotten here sooner, say . . . about *ten minutes ago*. Nathaniel and Serena, are here already," she said pointing.

"Uh-huh, no worries, honey. I've got a li'l something, something for Mr. Jackson. How dare he use me for his own selfishness, as if I don't have any feelings?" Melissa seethed, forgetting all about her earlier happiness. "There will be no more of him hiding his infidelity with me from Serena, and I mean that. Now, let's try to enjoy the service as my man's mother-in-law comes and preaches a sermon that will make folks wanna stop lying, dipping, and diving . . ." Melissa whispered.

"Humph! Did you hear what you just said?" Trina asked. "Maybe I'm hearing things because you are the biggest infidel in this church. I guess the Word of God doesn't apply to you, since you have done the *very* things He speaks against. Now you want to ruin someone else's life because you couldn't let go and send Nathaniel away instead of welcoming him into your home and bed," Trina said. She loved her best friend, but she knew that Melissa had some serious issues, and that she hated losing.

"Shh." The usher looked at them both with disdain and walked on, waving fans in the air for those who may need one.

Melissa couldn't wait until the service was over. She really didn't care what else happened during the service since she'd missed the majority of her favorite part anyhow, praise and worship. She burned with anger as she thought about what Trina said. She wouldn't take all of the blame for what happened between Nathaniel and herself. It took two to tango, and he knew that she would take him in the first time he showed up.

It wasn't totally her fault that he kept coming and coming until recently. She had to admit that her motives for attending Abiding Savior had nothing to do with getting close to God. She was there to find a man. Nathaniel happened to be that man, and she refused to be second to Serena any longer. Melissa couldn't wait until the benediction.

If anyone had asked Melissa what the sermon was about, she'd fail the test miserably. She hadn't taken any notes, and she hadn't given one amen throughout the service. It didn't matter though because Trina was there hollering and shouting loud enough for their whole pew. As they stood to raise their right hands as the benediction went forth, Melissa's mind was on one thing and one person only.

"I'd like to do something a little different today, if I may," Pastor Sampson said catching most of the members off guard. There was no doubt that they looked peeved that she was adding something else to the already drawn out service, but Crystal was never afraid of their faces as she continued to speak. "I want everyone to go to three people and tell them you love them and prophesy to them that everything they are going through now God is going to turn it around for them."

Melissa whispered to Trina. "Is she serious? We are only two rows behind the two lovebirds, and I'm not trying to give Serena a hug or tell her anything else because I'd be lying."

"Girl, can you get over yourself just for five minutes and submit to the pastor? A little kindness ain't never hurt nobody. Who knows? This may be just what you need to be able to think about all the wrong you and Nathaniel have done," Trina urged.

Melissa didn't get a chance to recover from the question before she saw Serena and Nathaniel coming right toward her. Perspiration snaked its way down her back, and her palms were getting slick, even though she rubbed them together and tried not to look uncomfortable.

Serena sucked in a huge breath before she walked into the lion's den, hoping that her extending of the olive branch would give her some peace about the vision God showed her. She stepped into Melissa's line of sight and forced a smile. She reached out to hug Melissa before speaking, "Whatever you are dealing with, God is going to work it out for you." Serena held onto the stiff woman as she stared into Nathaniel's handsome features, silently questioning him of his latest disappearing act. "Melissa, despite everything that I know about you, I love you with the love of the Lord," Serena whispered into her ear and let her go.

Nathaniel avoided Melissa's gaze for as long as he could, but he moved into Melissa's personal space as Serena moved on to share the love with some others. "Well, Nathaniel, where have you been?" Melissa asked, holding onto him causing him to squirm.

"I've been busy, Melissa," Nathaniel said trying to break free of her grasp before Serena came back around and went off on both of them. She'd been saying things lately that let him know that she knew that he'd been spending time with Melissa. He didn't need or want the headache of trying to explain himself. Passersby walked by bumping into him and pushing Melissa closer to him as they took full advantage of the fellowship.

"You've been avoiding me, but after today you won't be able to avoid me any longer," Melissa said and smiled as she walked on to the next parishioner to speak life to. After church service was over, Melissa silently thanked God for stepping in and making it possible for her to be able to speak to Nathaniel. It didn't go quite the way she had rehearsed it, but God took care of it. Instead of waiting around, she grabbed her Bible and headed for the back exit. She wanted to avoid Pastor Sampson and the chance of running into Serena again.

"Whoa, where's the fire?" Trina grabbed Melissa's forearm, slinging her back around so that they stood face-to-face.

"Girl, I gotta get out of here. I'm going to give Nathaniel the great news," Melissa said, smiling like she'd won the lottery.

"Was the annoyed look on his face an indication of your good news? What did he say when you gave him a bear hug instead of the customary church hug?" Trina sneered at her best friend, not believing that she was determined to continue pursuing Nathaniel despite their little talk earlier.

Melissa hadn't told Trina of her pregnancy yet because she wanted to tell Nathaniel first, but she decided to share her news with her best friend. "Come with me, girl," Melissa said half dragging Trina to the nearest ladies' room outside of the sanctuary. Once they were in the bathroom, Melissa looked under each of the four stalls before exhaling and sharing her secret.

"What in the world are you acting so crazy for? You darn near pulled my arm out of the socket. All you had to do was tell me that you wanted to talk to me," Trina said rubbing her sore arm. She was sure there would be a bruise marring her buttermilk skin by morning.

"I'm sorry, bestie, but I am so excited about my news. I didn't want to say anything just yet, since I hadn't share the news with Nathaniel," Melissa said.

"What does he have to do with anything? You are going against the best friend code. I thought that we were supposed to tell each other everything. Now, if this is such great news, then why would you want to share it with Nathaniel out of all people before informing me?" Trina pouted.

"Look, don't act like that. I had every intention on telling you, so do you want to know what's up or nah?" Melissa leaned against the sink and watched the door.

"Duh, you'd better tell me since I almost lost an arm trying to dodge through folks just to get in here. What's the tea, girl?" Trina mustered up some enthusiasm.

Instead of speaking, Melissa reached into her bosom and pulled the stick out of her bra and placed it on the sink in front of Trina's face. She moved over and smiled so hard that her face could've cracked.

Trina's eyes grew two sizes bigger than they should have been. She covered her mouth in disbelief at what she was looking at. Tears sprang forth in her eyes, and she dropped her head to the floor. Shaking her head, Trina seemed to be in disbelief. Finally, she was able to find the words she felt she needed to say to her misguided best friend, "You're pregnant? How could you allow this to happen?" Trina wagged the pregnancy stick around in front of Melissa's face. "Don't you have any shame? We all have to go to this church, for Christ's sake. Have you even *thought* about how this is going to affect

Prophetess Serena, Pastor Sampson, or Nathaniel? Ann-ndd . . . You are supposed to be on birth control." Trina ran to the bathroom door and looked out to make sure no one was eavesdropping on them before speed walking in Melissa's direction.

Melissa didn't want to hear that, and she said so. "See? *That's* why I didn't want to tell you. You of all people should be happy for me, but instead, you're judging me. I'm almost 100 percent positive that once Nathaniel finds out about the baby, he will do the right thing by me and leave Serena." Melissa picked the stick up, turned around, and looked at her reflection in the mirror. "This baby will have a good home, and knowing the type of man Nathaniel is, I'm sure that he'll want to do the right thing," she said smugly as she reapplied her lip gloss, smacking her lips.

Trina shook her head at Melissa before speaking. "The right thing? What does either one of you know what's right since you are indulging in all of the wrong things?" she asked.

"Look, I know what I'm doing, okay?" Melissa gathered her things and blew a kiss at Trina before running out the door, nearly knocking Felisha down. She didn't even look back or apologize for blowing by like a tornado.

"Well, *excuse* you," Felisha said with a look of disgust on her face as she watched Melissa disappear down the hallway.

"Don't mind her, she was in a hurry," Trina apologized for her best friend.

"Thanks, but there is *no* excuse for her rude behavior, although I can't say that I'm not used to her stankness. And to think, the benediction wasn't given but ten minutes ago." Felisha shook her head and said, "I'll be praying for her deliverance."

"I apologized for her and informed you that *my* best friend was in a hurry, so slow your roll on the slick comments," Trina said before walking out of the bathroom. She knew that Melissa had some serious issues, but she wouldn't allow anyone to talk bad about her in her presence and not stick up for her. The truth of the matter was that her friend needed more than prayer; she needed an intervention.

Chapter 8

Serena picked over her meal. She wasn't hungry for food, but her appetite was ravenous for answers about what she speculated was going on between Nathaniel and Melissa. She'd grown tired of acting like she didn't witness the lingering hug that Melissa had given to Nathaniel not fifteen seconds after she'd left the woman's side.

Serena didn't believe that their interactions were appropriate, and she trusted her instinct that the words exchanged had nothing to do with encouraging one another. Her fears were compounded when later that evening, Nathaniel would leave without sharing his whereabouts with her. When she demanded to know where he was heading, he claimed that he was going to the recreation center.

Two weeks had passed since that night when Serena had gone to the rec center to see if Nathaniel was there like he said. He had pulled another disappearing act one night after dinner. Serena wanted to know what was going on with Nathaniel because his cell phone would ring twice in succession, and then stop. Although he didn't go into their bedroom, he continued to burn a hole in the carpet going back and forth to the bathroom and peeping in on Serena to see if he could detect her mood.

Serena had heard the phone ringing and picked up on the pattern the caller had used. She knew in her heart that it was Melissa, but she didn't have the energy to get into an argument of denial from Nathaniel. As she sat on her bed, her heart raced, and she knew that he kept walking past their bedroom to see if she was paying attention to what was going on. She counted down in her head how long it would be until he left the house. It didn't take long for him to peep in and give her some bogus story about needing to head to the rec center to get one of the young boys' files to bring back to the house. He claimed that he was going to come up with a plan geared to help the youth get back on the right track.

Instead of responding, Serena looked at Nathaniel with her face screwed up and lips tooted out, which meant that she didn't believe him. She waited a few minutes for him to leave, and the anxiety building in her gut wouldn't allow her to remain still. "Ugh, I hate this feeling." Serena paced and wrung her hands over and over. "I've got to see if he's lying to me yet again. If I hurry, I can see if he's really at the center." Depression weighed her down as she trudged into her closet to throw on some jogging pants and matching jacket before spying on Nathaniel.

The place was dark and obviously still locked. It was evident that Nathaniel hadn't gone to the center like he had said. Serena sat in the parking lot waiting to see if he'd show up. After waiting for an hour, she cranked the car up and headed back home. Her mind was boggled at the state of having to deal with her insecurities of Nathaniel cheating and her most recent health crisis.

"Serena, what's on your mind?" Nathaniel asked the very next evening as they sat at the Lone Star Steakhouse, which was her favorite restaurant. "You've barely touched your food, and if my memory serves me correctly, you said that you were starving before we arrived. What gives?" Nathaniel was sure that he knew why she was shuffling the food around on her plate and looking like her world had ended. His thoughts went back to the previous night and the coldness in the atmosphere when he'd finally returned home. Nathaniel was sure that Serena was aware that he didn't go to the center, but he wouldn't be the one to confirm her suspicions.

"I'm just thinking about some things and trying to make heads and tails of what my thought pattern is . . . unless you care to help me out." Serena looked up from her plate for the first time since they'd gotten to the restaurant.

"What would you need my help for?" he asked before taking the last bite of his porterhouse steak. He needed to concentrate on chewing his meat so that he didn't succumb to an anxiety attack and choke to death.

"I've been quiet for a little too long, but not anymore. What I need is your help in figuring out what the deal is between you and Melissa Wright. Where have you been disappearing to when you leave home? Oh, and before you say that you've been tying up loose ends at the youth center, try the truth. I followed you to the center last night when you said you were going there, only to find out that you were nowhere in sight."

Although it hadn't been on the steak, Nathaniel choked on his water and tears came to his eyes. He couldn't stop coughing as the water snaked its way down the wrong pipe. Serena didn't lift a finger to help him, but she knew that she'd hit the nail on the head. She watched him squirm, but wouldn't wait patiently for too much longer, so she hoped that his fit would be over soon.

"Hmm, what's wrong, honey? Cat got your tongue or something?" Serena felt a rumble in her stomach, and even though her food had become lukewarm, she tore into it.

Nathaniel didn't know what to say, but he couldn't tell her the truth about Melissa. He couldn't expose himself to the woman he loved so dearly. He was still having trouble believing that he was going to be a daddy. He shook his head at himself as he attempted to respond to his wife. "Nah, I'm okay, I was just thinking," he said.

"What's there to think about, Nathaniel? How long do I have to wait for you to be honest with me about what's what? I'm not a fool, so please don't try to patronize me with some lame reply," Serena said in between bites of her salad.

"When did you start following me around?" he asked incredulously.

"What?" Serena asked, thrown off by his answering a question with a question.

"I said, when did you start following me around?" Nathaniel failed at trying to sound offended.

"Following you around? If I were following you around, then I'd have all of the answers and wouldn't be sitting here playing this cat-and-mouse chase game with you." Serena stabbed at her steak furiously.

"There's nothing going on with her and me. She wanted to make a donation to the center and because she also wanted to do some volunteering for the youth girls, I actually met with her for dinner. I mean, she blessed the center with a huge seed offering," he said almost choking again.

Once again he told a half-truth. Curiosity got the best of him when Melissa whispered in his ear that she had something to show him and so he showed up at her home just as she'd expected. Melissa wasn't so quick to forgive Nathaniel for transgressing her twice. When he got to her place, she met him at the door before he could even ring the doorbell.

She swung the door opened and presented him with the little plastic stick with a baby blue, yellow, and pink ribbon tied around it. He remembered hearing her say, "You're the daddy, now unless you want your precious wife to find out about our little bundle of joy, then you'd better make some serious decisions about our future. Now get out and don't come back until you are ready to be with me full time."

"Nathaniel, where are you? Hellooo! I'm waiting on some answers," Serena said while tapping her fork on her plate trying to get his attention.

All of a sudden Nathaniel jumped as he felt chills slithering down his arms. He could have kicked himself for ever getting tied up with Melissa again. "Um, did you say something, Serena?" he asked, trying to remember where he left off in the conversation.

"You said something about a seed offering for the youth center. Why couldn't you tell me about it when I asked you? Why did you have to lie about where you would be? Can you explain why you've been more absent than present lately?" Serena was just getting revved up, and she didn't have any intention of being quiet anytime soon.

Nathaniel stared at her with a blank look on his face. He'd never seen her act that way before. She was definitely in rare form tonight. Confrontation wasn't Nathaniel's thing. He was feeling like he was a caged animal being pushed up against a wall with no way to escape, but his betrayal caused him to fall back and succumb to Serena's line of questions.

"You know you never even asked me what happened when I went to the doctor's office," Serena said pointedly. "My mind is rapidly changing about you. I never used to wonder where you were or what was on your mind. I've realized these past couple of months that you aren't the same man I married. I may not have any proof right now, but trust and believe me when I tell you this, God is not leaving me blind about your mess. Don't think for a minute that I don't really know what's going on between you two."

Serena didn't realize she'd been yelling, but she'd allowed her emotions to get the best of her. When she looked around at the faces of the people staring and whispering about them, she dropped her head.

"Babe, I'm sorry that I didn't tell you about Melissa and the donation. I know how you feel about her. And I didn't think you would care about the impact that her money would make to help us down at the center. Things haven't been going so good down at the center since Chris went missing." Nathaniel rubbed his hands together under the table because he didn't want Serena to know he was lying right off.

"You're a liar, and I know it. I don't know why all of a sudden you need anything from Melissa Wright knowing that she hates the ground I walk on. She's always been jealous of the fact that you chose me instead of her. I will never trust that woman, and you are quickly losing my trust as well," Serena spoke quietly. She was on the verge of tears as feelings of anger and sadness collided.

Nathaniel didn't have a reply, but he knew that he'd better speak up before Serena became irate again. He didn't know how he would be able to tell her of his misdeeds because if he did, he feared losing her forever. "Serena, I've tried to be there for you time and time again, but you are only concerned about yourself. I love you with everything in me, but the emotional tirades have worn me down, and I've gotten fed up with it.

"I'm sorry for lying. There's never a good reason or excuse for it. I'm sorry for not being there when you felt like you wanted me around, but when I would try to show you that I'm here to fight through this thing with you, you don't waste any time showing me that you don't want to be bothered." Nathaniel's heart was breaking as he glanced at his wife visibly hurting as well.

"You say I don't want you around? Does that give you the license to leave home and lie about where you're going and who you're with?" Serena demanded to know.

No answer came from Nathaniel because he was out of words. He didn't know how to convince Serena that he didn't want things to turn out the way they did, but if he told her what he'd really been doing those nights he left her all alone to deal with the recurrent cancer by herself, his marriage would be over.

"Well, Mr. Jackson, since you don't have anything of value to say, I do. The doctors told me that not only did my cancer return and spread to my bones, but they also informed me after getting needed blood work, that I'm three months pregnant." Serena used her napkin to wipe the tears from her eyes and threw it down on top of her plate after delivering her startling announcement.

Nathaniel sat stunned. He couldn't bear to look at his wife. He was in a world of hurt knowing that he not only had one baby on the way—but two. The mental calculator started its addition of when he could expect to be a father—twice. Melissa was four and a half months along and would be due in December. That would make Serena due in January at some time. Feeling as if the wind had been knocked from his lungs, he needed to take a walk and get some space to gather his thoughts. "Excuse me. I'll be right back."

"Sit down, Nathaniel, because I'm not done talking to you. This baby, our baby's life, is at stake because of my illness. The doctors have advised me that I should have an abortion in order to get started on another regimen of chemotherapy. I refused because there are no guarantees of my going into remission again. I neglected to get help right away and have jeopardized my chances of healing this time."

Nathaniel wanted to walk away but hearing Serena's news about her decision to forgo treatments made him pause. Turning back around to face her, he asked, "What do you mean you refused? What are we going to do now? What are the doctors saying if you don't get the treatment, and why didn't you tell me? How come no one told me what was going on? I had a right to know as soon as you found out." Nathaniel was furious as the news hit him like a ton of bricks.

Serena watched Nathaniel as his chocolate facial features turned different shades of red. She focused on the latter which was anger, but in all honesty, he'd done that to himself. She spoke calmly, "You should have been there. I called you the morning after I got home from the doctor, but James said you'd stepped out and you didn't inform him of where you would be or when you were returning.

"So how dare you sit there and act like you were so concerned about me when you were out doing God knows what with Melissa. I waited up for you to come home that evening and the next few nights after that to have this conversation with you, but due to your late arrival each time, I'd fallen asleep. And, well, since you never inquired, I didn't feel pressed to tell you anything." Serena said defiantly.

Once again, Nathaniel had no rebuttal to offer. He'd been busted without verbally admitting to doing anything wrong. His silence nailed his coffin shut, and there wasn't anything he could do about it. His punishments for his act of adultery were being dished out tenfold, and Nathaniel didn't think that he would survive the fallout from what he'd just been told.

Serena wished in her heart that Nathaniel would say something or do anything to soothe her damaged heart and diseased body. He promised that he would always be there for her, but instead, he'd run at the first sign of trouble. She could admit that she'd been moody and mean more times than being nice to her husband. In all honesty, he'd tried to be her knight in shining armor just as he had the first time she had a bout with cancer. But unfortunately, this time wasn't like the initial diagnosis.

With her faith weakened, Serena just didn't believe that she would be so blessed to be able to stand before throngs of people and women all over the world to tell them how God had brought her out, not just once but twice.

"Since you have nothing to say, I'm ready to go home." Serena looked around for their waiter, and when she didn't see the young man with the sandy-blond hair nearby, she called out to the nearest waiter. "Can you find Jeff and tell him that we're ready for the check?" Serena got up and left the table, leaving Nathaniel behind to pay for the food.

Chapter 9

"Yes! Aw, baby, are you telling me that I'm going to be a grandmother?" Crystal began doing the happy dance around her kitchen while cradling the phone between her chin and shoulder.

"Mom, listen to me. That's not all I have to share with you." Serena paced around her kitchen, wondering how she would break the news to her mother.

Crystal had already begun to mentally plan her grandchild's baby shower, baby shopping, and spoiling her baby. "I mean, I can't wait to tell the congregation that we are having a new addition."

"Mommy, please let me finish," Serena whined.

"Baby, what is it?" Crystal stopped midjig and leaned over the stove to turn the heat down. She didn't like Serena's tone, but it sounded more alarming than disrespectful.

"Mother, have you forgotten the diagnosis of the return of the cancer?" Serena blinked her eyes rapidly to fight back tears.

"Well, yes, I do remember. I just got caught up with the talk of you having a baby. I'm sorry for jumping ahead of you. What does this mean for you? Will you both be okay? What are the doctors saying?" Crystal asked somberly.

"I don't know how to say this." Serena braced herself. "Dr. Sinclair and I went over the test results before she wanted a blood sample. Of course, it was a surprise for me to hear that I am with child. I mean, it couldn't have come at a worst time in my life. How could God allow this to be?"

"Serena, I don't know what to say, but you're talking slow, and I'm over here getting anxious. What did the doctors say?" Crystal plopped down in the nearest chair while she waited for the other shoe to drop with Serena's next words.

"I don't have many options, if any," Serena explained.

"Are you sure that this is what you want to do, baby?" Crystal walked back and forth through the house with the phone still tucked between her chin and shoulder. She was unable to sit still upon hearing Serena reveal that she'd been to the doctor and what the doctors told her during her checkup.

It pained Serena to have to tell her mother about the pregnancy because she knew that Crystal wouldn't agree with her decision to keep the baby and neglect her own treatments to sustain her life. So far, Serena was 2 and 0, but she held firm to her conviction which was not to abort her baby. Nathaniel had become even more distant since receiving the news, and Serena could do nothing about it because she had her own issues to deal with. After all, it was her life that was in jeopardy.

Crystal had been on pins and needles waiting for any news of Serena going to the doctor, and now she wished that she could rewind time to undo the call that would change all of their lives. She couldn't believe what she was hearing. She momentarily pulled the phone from her ear to look at it before replacing it, fighting to continue the conversation as she listened to Serena's decision to end her life for the sake of her unborn child.

"Mom, I'm at peace with my decision. If God is going to heal me, then it will have to be supernaturally if I'm to live because my mind is made up. I'm determined that my baby will live even if I don't." Serena sat at her kitchen table, bracing herself for her mother's reply.

Crystal closed her eyes tightly and shook her head. She wished that she was having a bad dream, but realized that she was in the midst of a living nightmare. "I sure wish that you would pray about this some more. What does Nathaniel have to say about this? Surely you have given him a chance to say his piece. Now, I know you two have hit some rough spots in your marriage, but what relationship doesn't go through good times and bad?" Crystal wasn't sure what to say to her daughter, even though she had counseled many married couples in her ministry.

"Mommy, I've made up my mind. What would you do if it were you?" Serena asked.

"Well, you know I don't believe in abortions; however, if it's to save the mother's life, then I may have to think twice about it." Crystal pondered the thought. "It just seems to me that you would want to save your own life because we all love you, and I can't stand the thought of losing you. That just seems like the better option because no one has become attached to the baby yet, so it would be easier to get over that loss." Crystal did her best to explain but felt that she was only rambling aimlessly.

"I can appreciate what you're saying, Mom; however, I never thought that I'd be able to have a baby. Yes, the truth is that Nathaniel and I are going through a lot of things right now, yet I still would love to be able to give him something to remember me by when I'm gone," Serena said.

"Please don't let this be the last time we discuss this. What mother do you know who would not try to change her child's mind from accepting a death sentence, when they both know the power of God?"

"Mom, I love you, and I want to thank you for your concern. I feel in my spirit that this is what I must do. I'm dying, Mommy, and we have to come to grips with the reality of this. If I give birth or I don't give birth, my body is too sick to recover at this point. I just want to live whatever time I have left with happy thoughts. I'm praying that I will get to hold my baby girl or boy before God calls me home, but if not, I'm good with what I have chosen to do."

"It sounds like you've thought long and hard about this. The only thing left for me to do is to stay in God's face, even though now it's harder for two of you. I don't need you being unhappy and stressed out during your pregnancy. I love you, daughter, and I'm here if you need me.

"One more thing, do you want me to let the church know what's going on with you or should I just make the intercessory prayer team aware of what's going on?" Crystal asked.

Serena thought before speaking. "Thanks for everything, Mommy. Please don't say anything to anyone, including the prayer team. I'd rather only the family know what's going on. That's why I'm calling each one of you personally so that if there are any questions, you guys won't feel the need to have to go around me to get the answers."

"Okay, baby, I will respect your wishes. I love you and will talk to you later," Crystal said.

"I appreciate you doing so, and I love you, Mommy. I'll talk to you later." Serena clicked her phone off.

Crystal held her cordless phone in her hands and screamed. Her shrieks were gut-wrenching, and the force caused her to fall to her knees. "Why, God, why does my baby have to die?" Crystal fell over on her face and cried out to God for what seemed like forever. Her heart was in great despair and turmoil. She didn't hear the knocks on her door or the doorbell ringing. She continued to cry out and beg God not to take her baby.

"Crystal, honey, what's wrong?" Tremaine stood looking in the window with panic written all over his face. He rapped his knuckles lightly on the windows in order to get her attention. "Crystal, it's me, Tremaine. Can you hear me, sweetie?" The more he called, the more anxious he became because she was in her own world, writhing on the floor as if she were in some sort of physical pain.

Tremaine pulled out his cell phone and called her phone. He heard the phone ringing as he peered through the window, hoping to get Crystal to answer it. She held onto the phone for dear life and ignored the shrill noise that emanated from up under her bosom. Eventually the phone stopped ringing, but by then, Tremaine had gone back to the door. Nervously, he rapped his knuckles on the wood door in a frenzy, hoping that Crystal was okay.

Crystal tried ignoring the doorbell and door knocking because she just wanted to lie there and cry out to God. She heard Tremaine outside banging on her door like some lunatic and knew that her nosey neighbors were already peeping out of their windows or even standing out on their porches trying to figure out what was going on over at her house. She crawled over to the couch and used its arm to pull herself up. She'd forgotten how hard it was to get up off the floor and rubbed her kneecaps before trudging to the back door where Tremaine was trying to knock it off its hinges. Opening the door, she fell into his arms.

"Crystal, what in the world is going on? I've been here for almost ten minutes and have been watching you wallow around, screaming on the floor. What happened that's got you all upset?" Tremaine held Crystal in his arms, and she felt his heart pounding against hers.

"It's Serena," Crystal sobbed uncontrollably.

Tremaine almost had to drag Crystal into the kitchen to the nearest chair. He sat her down and went to the bathroom to retrieve a washcloth. Returning to the kitchen, he ran cold water over the cloth and returned to the table handing it to her. Crystal's heart leaped when Tremaine held her. She had to admit to herself that she kept him outside waiting just to see if he'd leave or stay. It had done her heart good to know that he really did care about her. Crystal filled Tremaine in on the details of the phone call and couldn't fight her tears and the overwhelming feelings of sadness.

Careful to not scrape the floor, Tremaine picked his chair up completely and moved it closer to Crystal. Once again he really didn't know how to help her so he called on the name of the Lord. He took her hands in his and said a prayer for them. His prayer not only surprised Crystal, but it moved her as well. She actually felt a little better. She kissed Tremaine on the cheek and said, "Thank you for that. I see that I'm rubbing off on you." She smiled and switched chairs to sit on his lap. "Have I told you how happy you have made me since I've met you?" Crystal asked.

Tremaine answered with a kiss of his own, but it wasn't on Crystal's cheek. He kissed her on the lips, and she welcomed his touch, turning her insides to jelly. He knew that he loved Crystal and didn't want to lose her, but he also knew that if he wanted to remain around then he would need to trust his heart and ask her to marry him. They'd had many conversations about the possibility of marriage, but he'd sidestepped it each time because he wouldn't be able to take another heartbreak. He chided himself for thinking that Crystal would hurt him the way Riva did. It didn't matter to him that she was a woman of the cloth; he still had his doubts.

Tremaine held onto Crystal until his arms and legs were numb from her weight. "Baby, my body has fallen asleep," Tremaine said, wiggling his limbs. Figuring she'd fallen asleep as well, he tried not to make any subtle movements because he didn't want to startle her.

Crystal had gotten so comfortable in Tremaine's arms that she had fallen asleep. His jiggling jarred her from her slumber. "Oh, I'm sorry. Did you say something, honey? 'Cause, I believe I fell asleep. Was I snoring?" Crystal asked, embarrassed. She had felt so comfortable with Tremaine, but she didn't want to drop her family issues in his lap. It wasn't like he'd solidified their relationship or said that he'd wanted anything more from it.

Feeling cramped, Crystal moved one leg at a time, and then stood upright to stretch her muscles out. She looked back at him and smiled. "Thanks for being a comfort during such troubling times. I love you, do you know that, Tremaine Whitted?" Crystal could hardly believe that she'd said it first. She'd always hoped that Tremaine would be the first to declare his love for her, but things were different than when she was growing up.

Tremaine wasn't sure if he'd heard Crystal right. Did she say she loved him? He shook his head as if in disbelief, and then a lazy smile appeared across his handsome features. "Wow, lately, I've been wondering if I'd ever measure up to be the man that you could love. I know I'm not in church as much as you'd like for me to be, and I know I can get wrapped up in my patients at the hospital, but I can honestly say that I never thought I was worthy enough of a woman's love," he said with tears in his eyes as he pulled Crystal back down onto his lap.

"Honey, we are all worthy of love." Crystal gladly sat back down and made herself comfortable. "No matter what your ex-wife did, you must believe that it wasn't your fault. I mean, don't get me wrong, there are no perfect marriages; however, God's Word says that what He has put together let no man put asunder. Now, I remember you telling me about what happened between you and um, Riva, is that her name?" Crystal acted like she couldn't remember the woman's name, but she did.

Tremaine nodded his head, letting Crystal know that she was correct.

"Well, I never thought that I would ever have another chance at love. So many times it probably could have come my way, but I was always too busy and mainly afraid. When we first met, something leaped in my spirit and that hadn't happened since my deceased husband passed. I can only pray that one day you will let your heart lead when it comes to you and me. I'm not a spring chicken anymore, and I'm not trying to be single for too much longer," Crystal said gently, and for the first time since Tremaine had arrived at her house earlier, she had a smile on her face.

"Miss Lady, I'm in awe of God. I'm just in awe, but I've been waiting for a long time to tell you that I love you. I've always loved you since the first time you spoke to me." Tremaine thought back to their first meeting when Serena was in the hospital for throat surgery. "Instead of saying hello, you asked me that if I died that night, did I know where I would spend eternity." Tremaine and Crystal laughed as they reminisced on their first meeting. "I could barely think about anything else but you after I'd left Serena's hospital room."

"I'm almost ashamed to say this, but I was enamored with you on first sight as well. Once you'd left, Amina teased me about our interaction. I was embarrassed about the butterflies in my stomach or the way my hands grew sweaty when I thought about you. It's been forever since I experienced those types of feelings. I'd memorized your easy stride, strong handshake, and your picture-perfect smile." Crystal rubbed her hands up and down Tremaine's arm.

"Aw, I never hear you being so open about the way you feel about me. It's refreshing, and your transparency gives me reassurance that I'm not the only one who feels this way. Thank you for sharing your heart with me, because I know that it wasn't easy for you." Tremaine kissed Crystal on her cheek.

"It's been such a long time since my first husband died, rest his soul. I never thought that I'd be in another relationship with a man. I was always too busy, but I was busy on purpose. One of the hardest things I've ever had to do was to sit by his bedside while he was on a respirator after having a heart attack and watching as the Lord took him home. I don't think that I could ever go through that again." Crystal shrugged her shoulders as a glimmer of sadness briefly appeared in her eyes, and then disappeared just as quickly.

Tremaine felt Crystal's body shift as she took in a deep breath. He didn't want her to worry about anything happening to him. It was his job to worry about her. "Oh, come on, now. I don't need you feeling sad. I don't plan on going anywhere anytime soon because we have lots of memories to make first," he assured Crystal with a gentle smile.

Crystal seemed to switch gears quickly as her mood lightened. "Yes, you're right. Thinking back caused me to get a little sad, but I'm good now. Where were we?" she asked, tapping Tremaine on the arm.

"We were just reminiscing about how we met." Tremaine smiled lifting Crystal from his lap. Standing up, he never let go of her hand as he gently pulled her into a full embrace.

Crystal relaxed and allowed herself to exhale. When she released her breath, she let the tension, anxiety, and fears loose into the atmosphere. Grasping ahold of Tremaine, Crystal had another good cry. She'd made up her mind that she and Tremaine were indeed built to last, and she thanked God for her good fortune.

Chapter 10

Melissa was nervous to go to the doctor and have the blood test taken to confirm her pregnancy. She'd been calling Nathaniel's phone nonstop for the last two days, but he had blocked her cell phone number. She'd gotten so upset that she'd began to experience some panic attacks and had to call Trina over to spend the night with her. Embarrassment of her behavior kept her holed up in her bedroom until it was close to the time to leave. Although Trina was her best friend, Melissa knew how she felt about her situation and had pretty much told her so. Once Trina was able to calm Melissa down, she preached at her and told her that nothing good would come from her trying to destroy Serena's happiness because of her thirsty ways.

Trina knew her way around her best friend's place. It didn't take long for her to cook up a hearty breakfast for Melissa and herself. When word of Melissa's pregnancy got out, she believed that she would finally win Nathaniel's heart, but Trina saw the destruction from the fallout that was sure to take place in the church and in her best friend's life. She shuddered at the thought of having to be there to help clean up the mess that would result from Melissa's trifling behavior.

She moved around the kitchen grooving to the song playing in her head, placing the omelets and bacon on three plates. Orange juice, coffee, and tea were on deck for each person's choice of drink. The table was set. Now, all Trina waited on was for Melissa to come out from the bedroom and their mystery guest to arrive. She said a quick prayer and asked God to forgive her for being in the middle of the mess brewing, but she was confident that God would understand her sticking by her girl in her time of need.

Melissa took her time getting dressed. Guilt weighed heavily on her, and as much as she tried to shake it off, she was unsuccessful. She may not have been very spiritual, but she'd sat up under Crystal's tutelage long enough to know that God wasn't pleased. Melissa imagined horrible things happening to her unborn child, and those thoughts burned like fiery darts. The only problem was that she didn't have a sincere bone in her body, and she hadn't stored up the Word in her heart in order to counterattack those thoughts. "Ughhh, I'm gonna go crazy," Melissa yelled into the empty room. She bent over grabbing her head as her voice echoed throughout the room and fell onto her unmade bed.

"Girl, are you all right in there?" Trina heard the commotion in Melissa's room and moved swiftly toward her bedroom and knocked on the door in rapid succession. When Melissa didn't answer right away she wrangled with the doorknob. The door was locked, and Melissa was in the room moaning and groaning. Worried, Trina tried to coax Melissa to unlock the door and let her in. The food, no doubt cold, was forgotten until the doorbell rang. Trina flew to open the door since Melissa was still locked up in her bedroom.

Looking out of the opened blinds, Trina saw Nathaniel standing there tapping on the door impatiently. She had half a mind to let him stand out there and wait. "Humph, I wonder what his problem is. He'd better be glad that I'm a decent Christian because my flesh is riding high on my back like a camel's hump on its back," she huffed, then walked toward the door to let him in.

"Well, what took you so long to get here?" Trina threw her hands on her hips with a scowl marring her beautiful features. "My girl is in there having another meltdown." Melissa stood back and allowed him walk in with a sheepish look on his face.

Embarrassment stung Nathaniel's cheeks, and the heat caused him to try to relieve the discomfort he was feeling by rubbing them. "I got here as soon as I could. I've got a meeting to attend at noon down at the center with one of the families whose son is missing," Nathaniel explained. He couldn't believe that he was standing in Melissa's house waiting to go to the doctor with her when he wasn't even present to accompany his own wife to the doctor who was also expecting his child.

"Oh, I'm sorry about that. I hope that he's found and is okay," Trina said lowering her voice. She felt bad for that family, and it momentarily took her back to how her little brother, who had been missing for a day, was found the next day with his little seven-year-old body floating facedown in the river on the other side of the woods from where they'd lived.

Melissa emerged from her room with puffy eyes, surprised that Nathaniel was there. "What's going on in here?" She tried to keep herself together although she was surprised to see Nathaniel in her living room. She'd been trying to call him to no avail, and now, there he was standing live and in the flesh. Her heart did a little two-step in her chest that caused her to inhale deeply.

Trina spoke up for Nathaniel, who stood looking lost, saying, "I called him to let him know that he needed to be here for you this morning. It was a struggle getting him to man up and agree to come, but voilà, he's here." Trina presented him as if he were a prize.

"Hey, Melissa, how are you feeling this morning?" Nathaniel forced himself to ask. He'd left his mind at home with Serena. He hadn't been able to fully process all of the whammies that promised to pummel him if he didn't make things right. Nathaniel owed Serena so much more, yet his thoughts and guilt had held him captive and were slowly sucking the life out of him. For the sake of his marriage, he wanted to ask Melissa to consider having an abortion. It didn't matter to him that he was asking his fling to kill his unborn seed. Having to steal Serena's peace of mind and remaining joy by telling her that he'd gotten Melissa pregnant was something that Nathaniel couldn't allow to happen.

"I'm an emotional wreck, and I'm scared because I've never experienced all of the wacko feelings that go along with being pregnant," Melissa spat. "And not to mention that my child's father has left me alone to deal with all of this." She felt herself getting emotional again and turned to go into the kitchen, switching gears. "Bestie, thanks for fixing breakfast, but why are there three place settings?" Melissa asked, as her eyes darted from Trina to Nathaniel.

"Why don't we all have a bite to eat before we head over to the doctor's office? I believe that once you have put something in your stomach, you'll feel better. This breakfast was made with love for my new god-baby. Come on over here and sit down." Trina pointed to the chair she'd pulled out and directed Melissa to it with her eyes.

Trina walked around them both and said, "Nathaniel, you can sit here." She directed him to the chair on the other side of the table. She didn't want to put them too close together . . . just in case things got ugly.

"I'll stand since I won't be here long," Nathaniel said defiantly.

"Nah, I can't eat at a time like this. My nerves are all jumpy, and I don't know if I can look across the table at that man." Melissa pointed at Nathaniel who stood with his hands stuffed in the pockets of his tan slacks. She could barely look at him without feeling lust and anger jump together into her flesh.

"Well, if you won't be here long, then *why* are you here? I mean, really, you've been ignoring me, blocking my calls, and now, all of a sudden, you're at my house. I wasn't good enough to hear from to tell you that I needed you here, but then, you show up today as if you're doing me a favor talking about you won't be here long? What's with that?" Melissa hopped up from the glass table and ran back to her bedroom and slammed the door.

"I knew that this wouldn't be a good idea, but I really don't know why I'm here. She's right. I've all but tried erasing her from my memory, but what has happened can never be erased. I cut her off too late, when I should have left well enough alone, and now, here I stand." Nathaniel shook his head at himself.

Trina suddenly lost her appetite as well. She dropped her muffin and the knife she was using to butter it on the table and swiftly walked to where Nathaniel stood. She placed her hands on her hips and crooked her neck before speaking with disdain in her voice. "Let me explain to you why you're here since you're 100 percent clueless." She'd just about had enough of his cockiness for the nine months she was going to be in his face concerning her godchild.

"You, my brother, are here because you made a decision to cheat on your wife and hook up with my best friend," Trina spat. "You never should have fallen for the tricks if you couldn't bounce back. So, now, that we are here, you remember that." Trina struggled to control her anger.

"Look, I'm not going to allow you to continue to disrespect me, Sister Trina. I understand that I've done wrong, but I didn't walk into this alone. However, I'm still a married man who has many troubles, some I've brought upon myself, and some that are just my lot right now. I'm sorry that I keep messing up, and you're right, I should have remained faithful to my wife instead of creeping with Melissa. There's no excuse for doing what I did, and to keep from making the situation worse for me, I just don't want Melissa to have this baby." Nathaniel heard the words leave his lips, but he knew in his heart that he had no control over anything at that point.

No one heard Melissa reemerge into the kitchen until she spoke. "What about *me?* I'm the one who's loved you unconditionally, and now you want me to kill *my* baby to hide *your* secret?" Melissa paused to take a deep breath and exhale before continuing. "You must have lost your mind if you believe that I'm going to honor your request. So, you have some decisions to make, and you'd better come to your senses quickly," she said with venom dripping from her words.

"If you think that I'm just going to disappear, then you have another think coming. Either way, your little wifey *will* find out about us." Melissa dismissed Nathaniel with a hand wave and turned toward Trina. "Are you coming?" Melissa slung her pocketbook over her right shoulder and walked out of the house, leaving them both standing there with their mouths ajar.

Nathaniel walked out to his car without looking over at Melissa. He'd parked on the street as to not block her driveway. He watched as they jumped into the car, pulled out of the driveway, and zoomed past him as if he weren't standing there. His problems were mounting with each passing second, and he felt like he was drowning without anyone to talk to. He should have been able to turn to his pastor in times like these, but because she was his mother-in-law he knew that wasn't a good idea. He was drained of the life he enjoyed before indulging in the abyss of adultery.

Fear gripped him in the stomach, and he caught a cramp. He'd given up praying about the situations he was involved in because he had no say-so in either. It began to drizzle and Nathaniel needed to get to the center before his kids began to wonder where he was. He hopped into his car and sped off down the street, making a left onto Antioch Road. His phone rang, and since it was connected through his stereo system, he didn't have to pick up the phone. It was convenient to be able to just press a button to receive or make calls. Glancing at the dashboard, he saw that it was Serena calling and pressed the talk button on his steering wheel.

The traffic was light as Nathaniel drove to the youth center with a pounding headache. "Hey, baby, how are you?" Nathaniel asked, rolling his eyes upward, unsure what the conversation would bring.

"Well, since you left before I got up this morning, I've been calling you to see how you are feeling about our last conversation. By the way, where are you?" Serena rolled over to the puppy licking her in the face. She moved him over and glanced at the clock to see that it was eleven a.m. and waited for an answer, although she was quite sure she knew where he'd been.

"To answer your first question, I don't know how I feel about my wife telling me that she's willing to die from this cancer. I'm upset, sad, and I'm scared, Serena. Why would you want to leave me alone with a newborn to raise?" Nathaniel's vision became blurry and to keep from ramming into the back of another car, he pulled into the nearest McDonald's parking lot and parked.

The angst in his voice caused Serena's heart rate to increase. She sat up in her bed and really listened to what Nathaniel had to say. She was shocked, considering that she knew he was splitting his time between two women. There was no question in her mind that the two of them had been together because she dreamed it more than twice. "Nathaniel, please, all of those things haven't been worked out as of yet. I'm not dead yet, and only God knows when I will breathe my last breath." She wanted to be upset, but she didn't want her baby to feel her stress. "And you are already finding someone else to enjoy in your spare time," she blurted out before thinking about what she was saying.

Nathaniel couldn't believe what Serena had just said. "What is it that you think you know?" he asked, dumfounded.

Serena laughed out loud saying, "I guess you really don't know me so well after all, but trust me, my resources are infallible. I'm very much aware about what's going on, no matter that you have tried to play me for a fool. I've given you opportunity after opportunity to come to me and tell me the truth." Serena paused to listen for a response. There was nothing, just a dead silence so she called his name. "Nathaniel, are you still there?" she asked calmly. She'd known he was still on the call because she didn't hear a click, nor did she hear a crash, so he was still alive.

"I'm here," he barely whispered. His life had totally spiraled out of control, and there was nothing that he could do about it. He'd never taken Serena for a fool; he was only guilty of mishandling their marriage. "All I know, Serena, is that I love you, and I'm afraid of losing you. I am struggling with all that's going on with you and us," he said, turning his car off.

"Mister, you sure do have a funny way of showing me your love. I didn't call you to argue; it's just that I'm an emotional wreck. Being pregnant and having thoughts of these being my last days has really done a number on me. And the least you can do is act more concerned than you have been and just be there for me," Serena rubbed her hands through her short Afro. She'd decided to wear it au naturel after the cancer.

Nathaniel didn't have the guts to confirm anything his wife had said. Instead, he whispered, "I'm sorry that I haven't been there for you. It just seems like you've got it all figured out while I'm still trying to figure it out. I know you're hurting, and I'm hurting too. Never did I think that I would lose you to cancer. I can't believe that God would do that to me after taking my mother. I've been running from you, the prognosis, and everything. I just pray that I can right the wrongs I've done with the time that we have left together." A tear dropped from his eye.

"Yes, me too. Well, I'm going to get off of this phone and feed Tango." Serena sat straight up.

"Serena, have you eaten this morning?" Nathaniel asked warily.

"Not yet. I'm just getting up, and I'm not hungry. I guess I'll fix a salad or something later," she said stretching.

"Well, you know where I'll be if you need me for anything," Nathaniel said, hoping that she wouldn't have a smart reply.

"I believe I'll be fine, but if I need anything I'll just call my mother or Amina. I know you have a busy day ahead since you're late for work."

Nathaniel sighed and looked out of the window at the traffic. "All right then, I love you and will talk to you later."

"Uh-huh, love ya too, and we will talk later," she replied before clicking the phone off on her end.

Chapter 11

Amina had been trying for weeks to spend time with Serena, but every time she'd called, Serena was busy, or so she claimed. When Amina's phone rang early that morning, she was caught by surprise when Serena requested for her to come over. The last few months Amina hadn't felt connected to her aunt, and she was experiencing separation anxiety due to the disconnect. Serena had raised Amina from a baby and groomed her in ministry. Other than being Serena's armor bearer and spending a few precious moments with her, even those times had become practically nonexistent. It was no secret that Serena had been turning down many engagements lately.

Trying to balance herself by standing with one foot on top of the other, Amina tried to figure out what she would wear that day. Her mind wandered with thoughts of Serena and what was going on. She hadn't missed the hollowness in Serena's voice. Every word that Serena said, she spoke with such finality, and that frightened Amina.

Neglecting to clean up her room, Amina bounced around her apartment in a frenzy. Once she was dressed and had combed her hair, tying it up into a neat bun, Amina found it difficult to concentrate on doing anything constructive. She thought about cleaning her bedroom or washing the dishes that cluttered the counter and sinks in her kitchenette from the night before. However, thinking better of it, Amina scooped up her keys from the nook and almost ran from her apartment in a mad dash to get to Serena's house.

"Come on . . . turn green." Amina hit the palms of her hands on the steering wheel. She looked down at her cell phone a little too long because suddenly she heard a car horn blaring from behind her. She'd gotten caught up checking out her timeline and the craziness she saw of some of her classmates on Facebook. Her neck jerked upward, and she looked into her rearview mirror to see the driver behind her waving his hands around. She could tell that he was furious. She pressed the gas a little too hard, and the car lurched forward. Amina's heartbeat raced until she was in the normal traffic flow. Thoughts of Serena took precedence once again, and Amina's joy of seeing her kept her occupied for the rest of her ride. She had some questions of her own that she hoped would be answered.

Pulling up into the driveway, Amina barely had her car in park before she jumped out and ran to the house. Ringing the bell, she inhaled and exhaled to calm herself. Amina could hear the dog barking through the door, and soon she could hear Serena telling the dog to stop all that noise. The door opened, and Tango ran outside as if he'd been waiting all day to escape.

"Tango, get back here!" Serena hollered out.

"Auntie, I'll get him!" Amina ran after the dog, but he liked the chase and kept on running around in circles throughout the yard.

Hysterical, Serena screamed, "Please, get don't let him run out in the streets. I can't take reliving what happened to Fancy. Ugh, I told Nathaniel that I didn't want another dog. Why can't he ever listen?"

Amina was finally able to catch Tango and get him into the house, but not before running herself crazy. She knew that she needed to exercise more, but she didn't realize she was totally out of shape. Inside, Serena filled Tango's water bowl and food bowl while Amina fixed herself some of her favorite sweet tea.

After cooling down, Amina said, "Auntie, let me greet you properly now." She stood and walked over to where Serena was sitting at the table, nibbling on a walnut banana muffin, and hugged her. "Auntie, I've missed you, and it's been too long since we've spent any time together. I'm glad you called me today, because I was beginning to feel like you didn't love me anymore."

"Baby girl, you know better than that. I've just been going through some things, and it hasn't been easy." Serena sat down and picked at her muffin, creating a mess on the glass tabletop.

"Tell me, Auntie, what's wrong?" Amina went back and sat down. She placed her hand on top of Serena's to stop her from tearing the muffin apart. She looked into Serena's eyes and noticed the dark circles that had made themselves home there.

Serena didn't know how to tell her niece that she may not be around for her wedding the following year. She dropped her gaze down onto the table and concentrated on using her pointer finger and thumb to gather the crumbs into a neat pile. "I have some news that I've been kinda keeping to myself, but I need to tell you what's going on," she said.

Amina braced herself for whatever the news was that Serena was about to share. She looked over at Tango to see him resting peacefully in his bed that was situated near the laundry room. She wasn't sure what was going on, and wondered if anyone else already knew that something was going on with Serena.

"Well, I have some good news and some not-so-good news. Which would you like to hear first?" Serena forced a smile on her face.

"I-I don't know, but I do know that you're scaring me, Auntie. Please, whatever it is, just spit it out," Amina said with a frightened look on her face.

"Okay, well, first off, you're going to have a cousin. I'm three months along." A gleam glimmered in Serena's eyes, and then quickly vanished. She rubbed her flat belly with little emotion.

Amina screamed excitedly. "Wow, congratulations, Auntie! When's the baby due? When do we get to find out if it's a boy or girl?" Amina rattled off questions so fast that she ran out of breath. She inhaled before continuing. "I'm so happy for Uncle Nathaniel and you. Oh my, is that why you've been so tired and moody lately? I mean, look at you. Your eyes look tired, and you hadn't really been hanging around for ministry meetings and stuff lately.

"You don't seem to be happy about having a baby," Amina said after examining Serena's face and demeanor. "I know you will make a great mother, and Uncle Nathaniel, he's gonna be the best dad. I just know it," she rambled on.

"I can't be happy about being pregnant because I've decided to forgo all cancer treatments," Serena said sadly. Tears pooled in her eyes as despair infiltrated her heart.

"Auntie, why do you look and sound so sad? What do you mean that you won't be taking the treatments? Won't the cancer spread if you don't?" The look on Serena's face caused Amina to stop asking questions. Her stomach quivered with fear as she waited on Serena to respond.

"I can't be happy because I'm going to die. I had to make a difficult decision to either abort my pregnancy or try another chemotherapy regimen, but due to the advanced stage of the cancer, I decided to allow my unborn child a chance at life." Serena whimpered. "I've been thinking about life and death a lot lately, which only makes my decision harder to stand by," Serena explained.

"No, Auntie, please tell me that this isn't happening I don't know what I would do without you. Oh my God! Why is He allowing this to happen?" Amina was overcome with emotion. "Does Gran-Gran know? What about

Daddy?" Amina jumped up and moved around the kitchen.

"Well, as I said I've had some tough decisions to make. The doctors have advised me that I should have an abortion in order to save my own life, and that I need to be back on another chemotherapy regimen as soon as possible; that seven and a half months from now may be too late." Serena looked at Amina with tears in her eyes.

"I'm so sorry, Auntie," Amina cried and went to her aunt to give her a hug. Serena stood to embrace Amina. She was the first person that she'd allowed in her personal space since finding out that she was going to die.

They held each other for the longest time until Amina felt like she'd cried her last tear. She pulled away and looked at Serena. Amina's eyes brimmed with fresh tears as she thought about how thankful she was to have Serena as a mother figure in her life. She couldn't imagine life without the woman who molded her into the woman she was. "Argh, Auntie . . . I can't handle this." Amina turned and walked into the living room.

Each time Serena had to tell another family member what was going on her heart broke over and over again. She didn't know what to say to her niece, but knew that she needed to finish telling her what was to come. "Baby, I've got to tell you everything today. I've decided not to have the abortion and to have the baby instead. I know that the cancer is widespread now, and I would much rather give my unborn child a chance at life knowing that even if I had decided to go along with the doctors, the chances are slim that the treatments can catch up to reverse the damage already done," she explained while tears poured down her face.

Amina fell to her knees feeling as if she'd never recover from the news she'd just received. There was no one to call, no one who could wake her up from the bad dream she'd wished she was having. Time passed by without a word between the two women. Finally, they ended up falling asleep on the chaise lounges. The ringing phone jarred Amina from her sleep. She looked over to see that it was getting dark outside and the clock read five p.m. Serena didn't stir although the ringer on the phone must have been set on ten.

"Hello, you've reached the Jackson residence. How can I help you?" Amina asked.

"Hey, Amina, is this you?" Nathaniel asked.

"Hey, Uncle Nathaniel, it's me. How are you?" He detected the sadness in her voice.

"I've seen better days, sweetie. Is everything okay there? James was kind of concerned since he couldn't reach you most of the afternoon. Neither one of us thought to call you there. I'm sure that Serena is happy to have the company, though. You know it's been awhile since we've had you over."

"Hmm, let me check my cell phone," Amina whispered, remembering that Serena was napping. "I'm not sure why I didn't hear the phone if it rang." She walked into the foyer to retrieve her purse and moved her hands around in the bottom of her pocketbook until she felt her phone. Grabbing it and hitting the power button, she saw that the phone didn't have any power. "Aw, my phone is dead. It was partially charged earlier today, but that would explain why James hasn't been able to get in contact with me." Amina walked back toward the kitchen. She glanced into the living room at Serena to see if she'd awakened.

"Where's Serena?" Nathaniel asked wondering why Amina was whispering.

"She's asleep, and I had fallen asleep too. It's been a rather emotional afternoon, and you know how draining that can be." Confident that Serena was still asleep, Am-

ina walked into the kitchen and sat down at the table to
continue her conversation with Nathaniel.

"Yeah, she hasn't been resting well lately." Nathaniel
didn't want to admit that he was part of the problem.

"Auntie told me about the baby." Amina paused for a
moment before continuing. "She also told me about the
extensiveness of the cancer." Tears streamed down her
face as she waited for Nathaniel to say something, but
silence was all she got. "Uncle, are you still there?" she
sniffled.

"Yes, sweetie, I'm still here. Just thinking is all . . ."
Nathaniel felt a sweat burst forth onto his face and on
the back of his neck. "Umm, did she say anything else?
I mean, did she share anything else?" Nathaniel silently
prayed that Serena hadn't told Amina about what she believed was going on between Melissa and him.

"Yes, she gave me the heartbreaking news. I declare, we
cried for about two hours before falling asleep. How do
you feel about the possibility of losing Auntie?" Amina
lay her head down on the table hoping to still the throb-
bing in her temples. She was on the verge of tears again,
but didn't want Nathaniel to feel any worse than he had
to already feel.

"Ah, I'm sure that had to be difficult for her tell you. I
know how close the two of you are, which is why she pro-
crastinated in telling you. I don't know what I would do
without her, and if there's a child to raise . . ." Nathaniel
allowed his words to dissipate into the air like a vapor.

"I just can't accept that this is happening. Does Gran-
Gran know? I mean, surely, she wouldn't just stand by
and allow Auntie to die," Amina said.

"Yes, she knows, and I know I can't nor will I ever be at
peace with what's going on right now." Nathaniel juggled
the cordless phone on his shoulder as he got up to close
the door to his cluttered office. He moved strategically

around the boxes full of papers and other informational paraphernalia strewn around the closed space.

The silence from both ends of the phone was deafening as Amina and Nathaniel retreated to private places in their minds. The vibrating phone startled Nathaniel, and he looked down to see who the text message was from. He stared down at it as it buzzed around on the tabletop. Glancing at the screen, he scowled and pressed ignore. "Well, kiddo, I've got to take this other call," he said.

"Oh, yes, I'm sorry. I was at a loss for words and thinking too much. Would you like for me to let Auntie know anything from you?" Amina's words were strained as her emotions lodged in her throat, determined to remain there.

"Ah yeah, let her know that I will see her soon, and I'll be sure to let James know that you are safe and sound," Nathaniel replied.

"I'll let her know and thanks. Tell James not to worry, I'll see him later on tonight." Amina remembered her aunt and uncle's situation, and it prompted her to say, "Uncle, I will be praying for you both. I love you, and you know how to reach me if you need me at any time. Is it okay for me to tell my dad about Auntie?" Amina asked, not wanting him to be left out of what was transpiring in the family.

Nathaniel stood up and leaned on his desk. "Uh, I'm not sure how Serena wants to handle your father. We don't want to do anything that may be detrimental to his sobriety. You know he's still dealing with everything that's happened, and it's not our desire to give him this information if it might overwhelm him to the point that he digresses back to drinking. So, for the time being, can you just keep this to yourself?" Nathaniel asked, anxious to end the call, but the questions kept coming.

"I understand what you're saying, but I believe that Daddy would have a serious issue being the last to find out what's going on. What I don't want to see happen is for this to divide our family since we've been working so hard to get things on one accord. I don't want to deter the healing process and restoration of each relationship involved." Amina stood to stretch her legs. She walked around the kitchen while waiting on Nathaniel to reply.

"Sweetie, you may be right; however, I'm sure that he'll get over it once Serena talks with him and explains why she waited to tell him. We have to remember that it wasn't easy for her to tell any of us about dying. I can't imagine life without her, as I'm sure you all can't either, but we have to let her handle this the way she sees fit. So, once again, please don't talk to him about it. I've filled James in on what's going on already," Nathaniel informed her.

"What? He knows? And I'm *just* finding out?" Amina nearly screamed out loud, not believing what she was hearing.

"Calm down. Yes, he knows, and I'm the one who shared it with him. I hope you can forgive him for not saying anything to you, but he's the closest thing I have to a brother, and I needed someone to talk to. I begged him not to share the information with you because I didn't want to rob Serena of telling you and the rest of the family in her own way." Nathaniel rubbed the back of his neck beginning to feel totally stressed out.

Amina was hurt because she didn't think it was right for James to withhold this type of information concerning any member of her family when he wasn't family. She exhaled while trying to keep herself in check. "Hmm, okay. I will be sure to tell Auntie you called, and we'll talk soon. Love you, Uncle." Before Amina disconnected the call, however, Serena entered the kitchen wiping the sleep from her eyes and yawning. Tango heard her voice and got up from his slumber. He yipped and ran around, nipping at her ankles.

"Hey, is everything okay in here?" Serena asked. "Ah . . . yeah," Amina replied, pointing her finger at the phone and said, "Um, it's Uncle Nathaniel, and he was just calling to check in. Did you want to talk to him?" Amina pushed the phone in Serena's direction.

Nathaniel heard the commotion in the background, and then the shuffling of the phone. He walked over to the door and peeked out of the blinds to see some of the kids running around and horseplaying. The buzzing of his cell phone caught his attention again. He figured that when he sent Melissa to voice mail the first time she called, that she'd be texting and calling until she got ahold of him. Dread filled his heart as he picked up his cell phone from his desk and saw the name of Malik highlighted across the screen.

Growing impatient with waiting for Serena to get to the phone, Nathaniel decided to disconnect his call, but as he held his finger to the END button, he heard Serena's voice on the other end.

"Nathaniel, are you there?" Serena asked. "Amina, I think he hung up. Didn't you just ask me—" Serena's words were cut short.

"Hey, Serena, yes, baby, I'm still here," Nathaniel said.

Serena was glad that he couldn't see her roll her eyes up in her head. Her skin ran up and down her back, giving her chills that momentarily resembled the pain she felt.

"I was just calling to check on you, but was surprised when Amina answered the phone." Nathaniel laughed nervously to lighten up the mood. He was resigned to the fact that nothing would ever be the same between the two of them now that his wife knew something even if not everything about Melissa and him.

"We're here, and everything is fine," Serena said unenthusiastically.

"I just wanted to let you know that I'd be home later on unless you need me sooner. I need to work on some things here after we close, and then, if you'd like, I can grab something for dinner." Nathaniel snapped his fingers as if the thought just dropped in his mind. "How are you feeling today?"

"I'm tired and irritable. Don't worry about bringing anything for dinner. I'll probably just whip up something here." Serena rubbed her hand through her curly 'fro. "You know what else? Don't feel like you have to rush home on my account. More than likely, I'll be asleep by the time you get here." Serena leaned backward on the counter.

"Baby, are you sure? I won't be too late, and I want to make sure that I keep you and the baby as healthy as possible for as long as I can," Nathaniel said, hoping that he would somehow be able to penetrate the walls that Serena had been hiding behind ever since things fell apart between them.

"Look, at least the baby will be fine. I'm doomed to die, and there's no need to try to deny it. Plus, I'm sure that someone else will have your attention if you don't show up there." Serena felt herself getting upset, more at her hard-heartedness than what she believed was going on between her husband and Melissa.

Tears welled in Nathaniel's eyes as he stared at the phone in disbelief that Serena had so easily dismissed him in front of company. His heart seared with pain. He walked over to his seat with pain etched on his face and defeat weighing him down. He leaned back in the ergonomically oversized leather chair and swiveled around so that if anyone was to come into the office they would only see his back. His head dropped as his thoughts ran a race in his mind.

Chapter 12

The phone buzzed again for the fourth time, snatching Nathaniel out of his gloomy thoughts. He didn't have to look at the phone to know who it was calling. His lean arm reached behind him and pulled the Apple iPhone into his large palm and placed it in his lap. Fishing his Bluetooth from his pants pocket, he haphazardly placed it in his ear, clicking on the button. Clearing his throat he nearly whispered into the phone, "Yeah, Jackson here." His voice was laced with disdain.

"I told you so!" Melissa spat into the receiver of her cordless phone as she sat at her kitchen table sipping on a glass of chilled Moët & Chandon. She wanted Nathaniel to dare her to prove the fact that she was indeed pregnant. His silence angered her, and she jumped up from the table almost falling. The heel of her Red Bottom stilettos got caught on the leg of her chair and although she stumbled, she was able to catch herself on the end of the table. The glass fell to the floor and broke into crystal shrapnel. Anger boiled in her belly as she lashed out and slurred, "You don't have anything to say over there, Misterr Jack-son?"

"What's with you?" he asked, dismissing the first piece of information she gave him about the confirmed pregnancy. His feelings were hurt by the conversation with Serena, and now his sorrow was being churned into anger at what sounded like a drunken woman who claimed to be pregnant by him on the other end of his phone.

"What do you mean, what's wit' me?" Melissa rolled her eyes although Nathaniel couldn't see her, and then said, "I'm calling my baby daddy to give him wonderful news, and he's acting like he don't wanna be bothered with me." Melissa whined as she kicked her Louboutins off and flounced down in the chair. "I'm celebrating for you and for me." Melissa pointed at the phone, and then turned her finger toward herself and poked her chest. "Do you know that a good glass of wine has just been wasted on the floor? Guess it's a good thing that my floor is clean enough for me to drink or eat off of." Melissa dipped her finger into the bloody red tonic and sucked greedily, making sure to magnify the sucking noise into Nathaniel's ear.

"Melissa, what do you want? I really don't care what you have going on over there at your house. And I don't have the desire or the time to sit here and listen to you abuse the alleged unborn child you're supposedly carrying. So you can miss me with the added drama. I have things to do and need to hurry up and get back to my business, so what's up?" he asked agitated.

"Oh, so now it's like that? Nathaniel, I tell you for not the first time that we are going to have a baby. You and me. We are preggos, and so you know what I want. You knew what I wanted the first time you came into the lion's den and lost your self-control. You've known what I've wanted since the beginning of time, and, baby, it's you. Can't you understand that I love you? I don't know how to explain it, but it is what it is. I promised myself that if I ever had any alone time with you again that I would maximize every opportunity to snatch you up," Melissa said, still licking the liquor from her fingers as if it were candy.

"I was a fool, and I should have never come to your home. If I could turn back—"

Melissa prepared to wild out on Nathaniel, fearing that his next words would be that if he could only go back, he never would have come to her. That night and the nights after that wouldn't ever have happened. She knew that he was getting ready to say that he'd made a mistake, but wouldn't hear it come out of his mouth. She cut him off. "If you could do *what?* Huh, Nathaniel? Wishing you could reverse this clock, don't you? Well, I've got news for you. The test results say you gon' be a pappy," she hissed at him.

Nathaniel stewed in Melissa's rants and mocking. His pulse raced, and he felt like destroying everything in his sight, but the reminder of the laughing kids in the bay area sobered him quickly. He couldn't deny to himself that he'd wanted the pregnancy scare to be a fluke, but now that he was obviously going to be a father to not one but two babies, all he could do was shake his head at himself. "Melissa, what else do you have to say? You've obviously been drinking, which makes a whole lot of sense if you're supposed to be pregnant. I've got other things that need my attention," he yelled.

"Yeah, something needs your immediate attention, and it's not what you think it is. I know that I've threatened before to let the baby news begin traveling so that it would be sure to get back to Miss Serena, but it seems that you're calling my bluff. So I guess it looks like I'm going to have to show you that I mean business, beginning with a meeting with Pastor Sampson. I'm sure that she'd be interested to hear what I have to say. You know, I can play the role of a drama queen when need be, and I am sure to gain the pity of the true saints at Abiding Savior," Melissa hiccupped, believing that she had Nathaniel where she wanted him.

"No matter what you do, there will be no you and me. I need for you to get it through your head. Baby or not, I'm married to Serena, and I do love my wife." He struggled to keep emotion from making him come across as weak.

"So what? You think that you're going to be able to hold on to your precious wife who you love so much when she finds out about our love child?" Melissa giggled into the phone, even though her heart was sinking as Nathaniel continued to deny her.

"I guess we're just going to have to find out, now, aren't we?" Nathaniel growled into the phone, and then clicked the END button on his cell phone. He could no longer hold himself together. "I've gotta get out of here," he said a little too loudly.

"Yo, bro, what in the world is going on in here?" James burst into the office without knocking.

"Man, the kids could hear you outside in the bay area. Look out there." James pulled Nathaniel over to look out the blinds.

What Nathaniel saw saddened him. Feeling ashamed, he looked at the kids who had stopped playing and stood still, staring in his direction as if in shock. The longer he stood there, the more intense the moment became. Nathaniel broke down crying because his world was coming to an abrupt end, and he really didn't know how he could fix the mess that he now wallowed in.

"Bro, I'm sorry, man. I know this can't be easy for you with the thoughts of the possibility of losing Serena," James said, closing in on Nathaniel to give him a hug. He drew the blinds shut and closed the door with his foot.

Nathaniel latched onto James and released his feelings of pent-up despair and anguish. James gave him time to get himself together, and then released him. Minutes went by and the only sound that could be heard was the ticktock of the old clock that had stopped telling time long ago. Finally, Nathaniel looked up at the clock to keep from looking at James. His face was flushed from the tears he'd shed, and instead of feeling better, all he wanted to do was go someplace and sleep until the nightmare ended.

James looked at his brother and knew in his spirit that there was more to the story by the way Nathaniel had been acting lately. Not to mention the unknown woman who called at all times of the day looking for Nathaniel, but would never leave her name or a message when he wasn't available. He knew he was reaching, but he couldn't put all of the pieces together on speculation alone. "Man, you can talk to me, ya know? I know that something has been going with you, and it's more than what you've shared with me concerning Serena." James stood and tried walking around, but there was little empty floor space as the office was crammed full of boxes of paperwork and other gadgets. He moved back to a safe place near the door and leaned back against it.

"I don't know what you're trying to imply. I mean, you know what's going on with my wife, bro. That's enough to make anybody lose it. Seriously, you think about it. What if Amina was sick, and there was nothing you could do to help her? What if the only way she could possibly have any kind of life to live was to abort the one child that God had blessed her womb with? I have no say-so in anything, I'm losing my wife, man. She's gonna die, now how do you think I should be handling *that?*" Nathaniel stood and slammed his fist down on his desk. He stared at his friend with bloodshot eyes.

James listened to everything that Nathaniel admitted, but he was still thinking about the one thing or person who he left out of the equation. Time was of the essence, and he knew that he'd have to ask Nathaniel who the woman was, and was she also the reason for his stress. James wasn't quite sure how to ask his boss and mentor, so he just blurted it out by saying, "Who is she?"

"What are you talking about, man? Have you been listening to *anything* that I said?" Nathaniel asked in disbelief, wondering what James was getting at.

"I think you know exactly what I'm talking about. I know how much you love Serena and vice versa. There's no way in the world you are walking in a daze every time I see you if something wasn't amiss." James scratched his chin as if in deep thought and said, "Nothing should be able to keep you away from Serena, knowing she needs you now more than ever, man. I mean, unless there's another factor in the mix," he said, hoping that Nathaniel would come clean with him.

"So what are you trying to say? Is there something that you think you know?" Nathaniel rolled his eyes. "And stop beating around the bush and just say it." Nathaniel's voice boomed, shaking the paneled walls. He trembled inside, fearing that James was going to expose his secret.

"Look, bro, I'm not going to sugarcoat this for you. I don't know where the disconnect came from between you and Serena, but I know that there's another woman." James looked directly into Nathaniel's face.

"Where'd that come from?" Nathaniel asked incredulously.

"A woman has been calling here the first thing every morning and throughout the day, demanding to speak with you. Now, unless you have some sisters that I don't know about, then there's another woman involved. Question is, what does she want with you?" James choked back the bile creeping up to his throat from the nausea that he felt in the pit of his being.

Nathaniel thought long and hard before responding to James's accusation. Silence once again filled the room as he struggled internally. Afraid to admit the truth to James because he knew that James looked up to him, he also knew that James expected him to do the right thing.

Before James started dating Amina, Nathaniel promised to show him how love was supposed to go.

Not wanting to confess to his friend and mentee that he'd failed miserably, Nathaniel tried to slide by James in order to get out of the office.

"Ha, I know you don't think that I'm just going to let you leave before confirming or denying my suspicions," James said in aggravation as he leaned over to grab Nathaniel's arm before he could escape.

Nathaniel didn't have any fight in him. With his back turned to James he sighed before saying, "I cheated on my wife with Melissa Wright from church, and now she's pregnant. There! Are you satisfied? The mystery is solved." Nathaniel threw up his hands in surrender. "You happy now, man?" he asked, more upset with himself for feeling that he couldn't handle his own issues than the fact that he'd broken the trust of the ones he claimed to love the most.

James started to speak, but before he could open his mouth to say anything, there was a knock on the door. Ill equipped at what his next words should be or if he was supposed to say anything at all, he welcomed the intruder—until he realized that it was that lady from church. Opening the door, he looked the woman up and down and shook his head before leaving. "Boss, I'll be right out here if you need me," James said, eyeballing the pair as she clumsily moved into the room.

"Hey, baby daddy, did I interrupt something?" Melissa swerved around Nathaniel until she stood at his side. Inches away from his face, she could tell that something had been going on between the two men before she arrived.

Nathaniel didn't realize he was clinching his fists until he felt pain searing into his flesh.

Unfazed by Melissa's presence, Nathaniel slowly loosened his hands and rubbed them. Without looking at her, he moved away from her and sat down at his desk. He stared at Melissa with hatred in his eyes. "Why are you here?" he demanded.

"Well, you didn't have enough time to talk to me on the phone, so I figured I'd find you here and decided to come down so that we can finish our discussion," Melissa said slowly. The effects of the wine she'd consumed earlier had her feeling discombobulated. "Aren't you going to ask me to sit down?"

Melissa twirled around in front of Nathaniel, hoping for a reaction. She twirled again and lost her balance, falling onto the couch. "Whew, I'm sure glad that I didn't fall and hurt our baby. You didn't even try to catch me to break my fall. Humph, you'd better be glad that I didn't harm myself, mister. I'd have to shut down this little business of yours," Melissa sneered, looking around in disgust.

"Once again, why are you here, Melissa?" Anger built up in Nathaniel. His mind told him to choke the life out of her, yet he knew that she was there because of him. His thoughts went to Serena, and he shivered inside. Although it wasn't the norm for her to come down to the center unannounced, Nathaniel feared that this would be the day she would come. Serena possessed a prophetic gift and didn't have a problem reminding him that she and God were on first-name basis.

"I've told you why *I'm* here. I need to know what you are going to do about *this*." Melissa stood up, pointing toward her belly.

For the first time since Melissa walked into the office, Nathaniel really looked at her. He noticed that the diva that had attracted him so many times before now looked a hot mess.

He couldn't believe that she had let herself go. Melissa's hair had been her pride and joy, but by the looks of it, she hadn't combed it in days. She looked tired and frazzled, as if should the wind blow too hard, then she would fall over. The shine that usually rode high on Melissa's skin seemed to have taken a hiatus and left a lackluster hue in its place.

Nathaniel couldn't believe that she was the same woman he'd abandoned his marriage vows for. Smacking himself on the forehead, he tried shaking some sense into it that would clarify how he allowed himself to get raveled into the sinful mess that she represented in his life.

"Well, what are you going to say now that I'm here in living color?" Melissa asked. "Are you going to give me what I want, or am I going to have to set up some counseling sessions with Pastor Sampson? You see, one way or the other, I *will* have you. I don't have any issues with telling your mother-in-law all about being lied to and manipulated by my baby's father. I will let her know that I loved my baby's father, and that he led me to believe that he loved me until I told him I was pregnant."

Nathaniel rubbed the fold out of his pants leg before pulling himself up to his desk and resting his folded hands on top. For the first time, he looked Melissa in her eyes and was taken aback. The jagged picture before him showed how broken the woman was. Ordinarily, Melissa came across to be as hard as nails, but Nathaniel saw that she was actually capable of showing genuine emotional distress. Her eyes were bloodshot, puffy underneath, and dark circles rested on the tops of her cheekbones.

"Melissa, you can't come prancing down to my place of business where I mentor many impressionable kids whenever you feel like it, talking about you're pregnant with my child. It just doesn't look good, and heaven forbid that my wife comes down here and finds you here looking like . . ." Nathaniel threw a hand gesture toward her, and she immediately bucked into his face.

"How *dare* you tell me where I can go? I don't care *nothing* about your wife," Melissa sneered looking psychotic in Nathaniel's direction. "That's *your* issue, not *mine*," she said.

Nathaniel realized that he was dealing with a ticking time bomb and that frightened him just a little. Melissa undoubtedly had Nathaniel's attention because he wasn't sure what she would do or say next. Leaning backward, Nathaniel wished that James would come in and dismantle whatever havoc was sure to take place if he couldn't deescalate the situation at hand.

"What's wrong now, cat gotcha tongue? Huh, baby daddy? See, if you would have listened to me and helped me to deal with this pregnancy, I wouldn't be traipsing around town looking like I just climbed off out of the trash heap. You've driven me to drink, and it's not good for the baby, or do you even care?" Melissa knew the tears were going to come, but she refused to cry in front of Nathaniel. He didn't flinch when her spittle landed on his face and chin due to her words flying at him like darts.

Nathaniel fidgeted in his chair as he could distinctly hear Serena's voice over Melissa's incessant verbal blows. Although the blinds were closed, he could still see between the slivers of space where the window ended and the wood paneling on the door started. Suddenly, his eyes grew to the size of baseballs and moved in sync with his racing pulse as sweat beads popped out on his forehead.

Serena moved closer to the office door, and Nathaniel knew that in a moment, his life would be torn into fragments of utter destruction. Before he knew it, Melissa had moved around to where he was sitting and lifted her hand in the air. Before she could unleash her frustration at him for his lack of compassion, the door flew open.

Serena rushed in with Amina and James on her tail. Serena took in her surroundings and the thick atmosphere, which caused her breath to catch in her throat. She coughed and Amina held onto her aunt until she calmed down. James eyed Nathaniel, saying nothing verbally; however, his eyes let him know that he was helpless.

"We've got this, James." Amina snapped her lips and pushed him toward the opened door. As James passed by her, she said, "Go back out there and make sure that the kids are okay in the front." Then she closed the door behind James, making sure it snapped loudly enough to get Melissa's attention as well. Leaning on the door, Amina placed her hands on her hips waiting for someone to break the ice.

Nathaniel sprang up from his desk, nearly knocking a wide-mouthed Melissa off balance in his urgent need to explain himself and what was going on. "Serena, baby, what are you doing here?" he stammered, feeling the blood drain to his feet. He didn't have anything intelligent to say and felt stupid as soon as the words popped out of his mouth.

"Yeah, what are *you* doing here?" Serena gave Melissa her full attention as if Nathaniel was a mere mirage and she could see straight through him. The anger was building inside, causing her to cough uncontrollably.

"Auntie, are you okay?" Amina looked around nervously for something for Serena to drink.

"Uncle, can you get something to drink for Auntie, please?" Amina's eyes darted between her aunt and uncle, wondering about what was soon to unfold. She'd wondered why Serena had been acting strangely after the phone call with Nathaniel.

Serena tried her best to get rid of Amina at the house, but she had refused to leave her there alone. The next thing she knew, Serena had asked Amina to drive her down to the center because she had a bad feeling and needed to check on some things. During the ride, Serena told Amina about her suspicions of Nathaniel cheating with Melissa. The news saddened Amina, and she prayed the whole ride to the rec center. Unfortunately, the very thing she prayed for went unanswered.

Nathaniel scrambled out of the cramped office space. The faces of James and the children playing in the play area of the rec center made him think twice about leaving the ladies in the office alone. He stepped backward into the office cautiously.

"Hey, man, can you round up some bottles of water for me in here?" Nathaniel asked James.

"Serena's in here choking, and I don't want the baby to be hurt," he said before closing the door once again. He looked around the room slowly, from Serena, who was being held by Amina, to Melissa, and back again. The room was pregnant with tension as Nathaniel waited for the fireworks of his last statement to spark the next conversation between the women. Anxiously, he waited for round one to begin.

Melissa cast Nathaniel a cynical glance, throwing her hands on her wrinkled jumpsuit. "Excuse me, what did you just say?" Melissa asked holding her hand to her chest, as if offended by what she'd heard.

"What's it to you?" Serena's coughing spell had ended, and she had caught her breath long enough to address Melissa for the first time since arriving at the center. She was in war mode as she stared at Nathaniel while directing her words at Melissa.

Melissa was ready to act a fool if need be. Instead, however, she returned Serena's hateful stare and said, "There's no way that you are carrying *his* baby." Melissa pointed at Nathaniel as if he was standing in a criminal suspect lineup.

"And *why* not? Does that sound strange to you? That *his* wife is carrying her *husband's* child?"

Serena advanced on Melissa, craning her neck to get her point across.

Amina moved slightly in front of Serena to shield her from an altercation that could possibly take place. She felt helpless when Serena nudged her from behind, and then bumped her out of the way to square off with Melissa again. "Uncle, aren't you going to do anything? What in the world has happened to you? You're standing there as if my aunt isn't about to check your girl," Amina shouted loud enough for James to come running into the office.

James came and stood guard, knowing that if anything jumped off, he'd be there to make sure that Serena wasn't harmed. He'd forgotten the bottles of water, but was relieved that Serena seemed to be okay.

Nathaniel tried to deflect by addressing James. "Man, where is the water? My wife could have choked to death in here waiting on you." He stood there looking frustrated over the entire situation.

Melissa wasn't moved by Serena's hype, nor did her bark frighten her. She stepped to the challenge and asked, "*Who's* gonna check me, boo?" She tried flinging her hair, but it didn't move. Rolling her eyes and turning her back on Serena, Melissa asked, "Nathaniel, is this woman pregnant by you or *what?*" Melissa leaned on the edge of the desk and waited for an answer.

"That *woman* is my *wife,* and you'd better respect her or else," Nathaniel spoke up finally, moving forward to stand at Serena's side and posted up.

"Your *wife?*" Melissa laughed like she'd heard the best joke ever.

"Did I stutter?" Nathaniel turned toward his wife with tears in his eyes, convinced that things would never be the same.

Amina moved out of the way, linking her arm in James's arm. "What is *she* doing here?" she asked James.

James didn't like being in the middle of the mess Nathaniel created. He was glad that the children's parents had come to pick them up and that the center was now empty. Amina nudged his arm waiting on an answer. "I don't know what she's doing here, and before you begin badgering me with questions, all of this right here is new to me." James pointed at the people standing in the room to get his point across.

"Well, we need to pray because Auntie Serena is sick and pregnant. I couldn't believe it when she told me about Uncle Nathaniel cheating. How could he abandon her when she needs him the most? I never would have thought he was this type of dude," Amina whispered, shaking her head.

Amina and James held hands, quietly watching the drama evolve as the disheveled woman addressed Nathaniel in a huff.

"You didn't answer my question. Is she pregnant with your baby too?" Melissa demanded.

Serena reacted before Nathaniel had a chance to. She stepped around him to get at Melissa. It had never occurred to her that Melissa could be pregnant as well, but it was becoming clear. Looking upward to the ceiling, Serena focused on the broken wooden tiles that had browned over the years and shook her head in disbelief. She felt helpless and hoped the roof would be removed from the building and that God would take her right then. Serena shook her head incredulously before taking charge at Melissa. "*Too?* So your purpose for being here looking like death warmed over is because *you're* pregnant?" Standing toe to toe, Serena stifled a cough.

"You'd better back up off of me or—" Melissa said taken aback. Once she'd had a chance to think about what was going on, she jumped right back into Serena's face. "Well, since your husband is having a baby with you *and* me, then I'd suggest y'all get ready to pay some child support." She huffed allowing her street ghetto side to show up and take control.

Any feelings Nathaniel thought he'd ever felt about Melissa went up in smoke. He wanted to reach out and strangle her until her body dangled lifelessly in his clutch, knowing he had to put an end to the foolish scene before he did something else he would regret. His heart pounded furiously with anger and fear. "James, get her out of here!" he said pointing at Melissa.

"Uncle, I don't mean any disrespect; however, you allowed this tart access to your life," Amina cut in. "I won't stand by and allow James to be pulled into this nonsense. If *you* want her to leave, then you will have to be the one to get her outta here." Amina grabbed James's hand again.

James let go of her hand and addressed Melissa. "Look, you've caused enough trouble here. Can you just leave already?" He stood erect, hoping that would deter Melissa from continuing her rant.

James could barely look at Melissa, fearing that he'd turn into stone by looking at the tramp. He even moved back to give her room to move in front of him and exit the office.

"I ain't going nowhere until Serena knows everything that Nathaniel and I have been doing behind her back," Melissa snapped, looking over her shoulder. "Now, Nathaniel, do you want to share with wifey what's going on, or do I need to?"

Melissa hitched her hands upon her shapely hips, determined to have her say by exposing her true feelings for Nathaniel. The opportunity had presented itself, and she had no intentions of covering up their love child, determined that once it was done and said, Serena would leave Nathaniel, and he'd be free to be with her.

"Get out of here, now, Melissa," Nathaniel ordered. "I can inform my wife on what's been going on between you and me. We don't need you embellishing the situation as if any of this was supposed to happen."

"Honey, the only thing that will be embellished is this right here." Melissa smiled and rubbed her flat tummy in circular motions and turned around slowly, making sure that everyone in the room knew what was to come. "I don't have to say too much except for this: I'm pregnant with your baby, and if any of you want to dispute this fact, I'll make sure you all are personally invited to the birth of the baby and watch the doctor perform the DNA test." Melissa's buzz had finally worn off, and she was acting out from her emotions. She felt compelled to divulge more intimate details of her relationship, to make sure by the time she left that center, Nathaniel would be eating out of her hands.

"To your point, all of this *was* supposed to happen. You pursued me, came to my house time and time again. It was obvious that you didn't respect your wedding vows, so I don't know why you are surprised that I didn't. Selfish of me maybe, but I allowed you to have all of me. There was no secret that I've wanted you from the day I met you, so wedding ring or not, I hoped that being with me would make you wake up and realize your mistake . . . of being married to *her*." Melissa allowed the tears to fall.

Before Serena could approach Melissa, Nathaniel jumped in between the two ladies moving at lightning speed. He didn't say a word, but his blood was boiling. He had never been so angry before. Nathaniel snatched Melissa by the arm, pulling her past Amina and James, out of the office into the front of the center. Once they were outside, he unleashed on Melissa as if she were the most despicable person he'd ever seen.

"Have you lost your mind? I've never known you to be ghetto fabulous. How dare you think that I would allow you to put your hands on my wife. You'd better leave my place of business before I throw you out of here," Nathaniel demanded.

"Let me go, you're hurting me!" Melissa snatched her smarting arm away from Nathaniel's grip. "No, I haven't lost my mind, but you've lost yours if you think that you are going to get away with anything. I promise when I'm done with you, you will wish you had *never* met me." Melissa looked past Nathaniel into the office at Serena who stared at her with pure hatred in her puffy eyes.

"I *already* wish that." Nathaniel mumbled rubbing his hands over his head.

"This is your last opportunity to leave her." Melissa pointed in the direction of Serena with her lips tooted up.

"That won't be happening—ever," Nathaniel responded slowly. He realized that Melissa was desperate enough to expose him to the church, and the fear of that gave him chills.

"So be it then. Have it your way, but know this, baby daddyyy, you *will* pay for breaking my heart, not once or twice, but three times. I bet you're wondering how I came up with three," Melissa taunted, and then began to count on her fingers, all the while peeping around the corner into the office to see if Serena was going to come for her again. Serena didn't move from the spot she was standing in, but she kept her eyes on Melissa just the same.

Nathaniel only wondered about what this intrusion had done to further drive a wedge between his wife and himself. "I'll ask you for the last time to leave my place of business and don't come back, or I will file a restraining order." Nathaniel mustered up all of the bravado he could to get his point across. He just wanted the day to be over, wake up all over again, and do it better the next time. But unfortunately, the only thing that looked like it was about to be over . . . was his marriage.

Chapter 13

Serena lay on the examination table with tears rolling from her eyes as she twisted her neck trying to see the monitor. The ultrasound wasn't going too well because her baby wasn't cooperating with the nurse who couldn't detect the sex. Nathaniel stayed by Serena's side holding onto her hand, mesmerized by the little image bouncing around on the screen. He couldn't believe that he was going to be a father . . . again.

"Everything seems to be in its right place." The nurse turned the monitor off and handed Serena a warm rag. "You can use this to wipe all of that goo off of your belly." She smiled.

"I'll leave you to get cleaned up. If there's anything else I can do for you or any questions you may have, please don't hesitate to reach out to me."

"I do have a question for you," Serena said.

The nurse turned around with a smile on her face, hoping that she could address Serena's concerns. She'd been prepped by Dr. Sinclair before being asked to do the ultrasound. "Yes, you can ask me anything that you want to, and I'll do my best to address your concerns."

"Is my cancer going to affect my baby? Is all of this for naught? I don't want to have to leave my little boy or girl struggling to live after I'm dead and gone." Serena confessed her fears for the first time to someone other than her mother.

"Baby, try not to think the worst. Everything will be fine. I believe that God will turn this situation around the same way that He did before." Nathaniel stepped in to reassure Serena. He wanted to be the positive force in the room. His heart broke over and over again at all the trouble he'd caused recently.

Fear had a stronghold on Serena, and she needed moral support even if it came from the one man she'd loved with all of her might until he betrayed her. Hearing his voice still gave her chills as it did when they'd first started dating. Her mind wandered back to the first time they met, and then to when she'd initially found out that she was positive for throat cancer. Nathaniel was always there, being attentive and loving her. Tears trickled down her face as she turned her head away from the nurse and Nathaniel, who was still standing there watching her.

"Mrs. Jackson, right now, we are watching you and your baby's health very closely. If we discover any abnormalities, we will let you know as soon as we find them. I don't want you to stress about anything. The less duress you are under will prove to be beneficial to you and Baby Jackson." The nurse moved toward Serena and rubbed her shoulder before saying, "I will leave you to get dressed if there's nothing else."

Nathaniel saw the pain etched on Serena's face and the furrow in her forehead. He nodded to the nurse and said, "Thank you for all that you've done today. If we need any more information we'll be sure to reach out to Dr. Sinclair."

Serena's tears turned into whimpers, and then into groans. She hadn't moved to wipe her growing belly off. Feeling powerless, she cried and cried, thrashing her head back and forth as if she were in physical pain. The pain she experienced wasn't physical; it was emotional. It rendered her weak and helpless.

"Baby, do you want me to get you cleaned up so that we can get out of here?"

Serena didn't answer right away; she stretched her arm out and beckoned Nathaniel closer. Emotionally spent, she never stopped crying. Tears fell for so many reasons, but Serena knew that she couldn't hold a grudge forever. Her thoughts were on her unborn child and how her baby deserved to have a fighting chance to be raised by two parents for as long as possible. Serena looked at her baby on the monitor and what she saw solidified her decision to forgive Nathaniel for cheating with Melissa. Her love for him was greater than his sin, and she wouldn't allow the tricks of the enemy to distract her from further fulfilling her God-ordained purpose in the earth.

Nathaniel walked over to Serena and grasped her hand in his. He wondered what was going through her mind as his was in turmoil and unrest. Day after day he wished that the hands of time could be rewound. Continuously, he scolded himself about his transgressions and how he would have to live with the outcome and reality of what was going on in his life. Tears trickled down his face as he contemplated losing Serena and having to raise their child alone.

Taking great care in wiping down Serena's belly, making sure to remove all of the gel, Nathaniel could barely contain himself. This was the first time since the incident at the center that Serena had allowed him into her personal space. He was afraid to say more than two words to her, unsure of what her response to him would be. After they'd returned home, she'd taken to her bed once again, and Nathaniel ended up having to give Tango away because Serena didn't have the desire to take care of him any longer.

"Serena, what can I do to make up for all of my wrongs to you?" Nathaniel asked as he lifted her to her feet and assisted her with getting dressed. Conviction caused his hands to tremble as he finally gathered enough courage to step to his wife. She was even more beautiful to Nathaniel than the day he married her. Determination drove him as he vowed to give her whatever she asked for every day that God granted to them.

"I only know what you can't do, and that is to erase the pain from my heart or the disappointment etched in my face, body language, and the loss of zeal for living," Serena said with sadness in her eyes. "I'm willing to let this go because if I don't, the fact that you felt the need to go and rekindle your relationship with Melissa will kill me before the cancer does.

"While I'm not accepting any blame in your decision to seek the comforts of another woman, I will admit that I didn't make things easy for you when I found out the cancer came back. I take blame in pushing you away and being selfish with my feelings and neglecting yours. Not knowing how much time I have left and what's going to happen when I'm not here keeps me up at nights, restless, and I'm sure that the baby is being affected by the stress."

"Baby, I don't have any excuses about what I did. I understand now that I should have just given you the time you needed to deal with your feelings. I should have been man enough to fall back until you were ready to deal with what was happening. Please forgive me, Serena. I need to know, baby, that you will give me a chance to make this up to you. I'm praying to God that He will give us more time to get this right. Please, baby, I'm begging you to let me love you. Knowing that I can't touch you the way I used to, hold you, and you feel comfortable lying next to me is killing me inside." Nathaniel looked at Serena with longing in his eyes.

Serena saw that he was suffering and had been for the past few months because of their selfish actions toward

each other, and she wanted to tell him that she had forgiven him already, but instead, she leaned over and gave
Nathaniel a soft kiss on the lips. A feeling ran through her
that she hadn't felt in a while, and that let her know that
she did still love him despite the hurt, lies, and cheating.
Yeah, right then and there she believed that God would
make everything all right.

Nathaniel took full advantage of the first sign of peace
Serena had given to him. He held her gently, but allowed
his desire for his wife to keep the kiss going for as long
as she would allow. They were engrossed in each other
when they heard someone enter the room, causing a
much-needed distraction.

"Oh! I'm sorry!" the nurse said as she turned her head
in the opposite direction. "I thought you had left already.
I really need to get in here to prep for the next patient."
The nurse blushed, embarrassed for the two of them.

"Please forgive us," Nathaniel smiled at the nurse as he
pulled Serena behind his back. "We'll get on out of your
way now," he said as he led Serena out of the door.

Chapter 14

Crystal had barely given the benediction before she was bombarded by Melissa. The pastor greeted her as she did every time she saw the woman, but she knew that something wasn't quite right with her. She hadn't seen Melissa in almost two months, and even though she felt in her spirit that trouble was brewing, because she was a member of Abiding Savior, it was Crystal's charge to be concerned about all of God's sheep. Melissa cried and thrashed around, visibly having some sort of breakdown. When she stood in front of Crystal, she spoke incoherently, which caused Crystal to motion for her armor bearer, Jalisa, to come to her aid.

"Sister Jalisa, take Sister Melissa to the back. She can wait for me there," Crystal instructed her armor bearer.

"Yes, ma'am." Jalisa took Melissa's arm and led her to the pastor's study. "Sister Melissa, is there anything I can get for you?" she asked, ignoring the billowy dress that Melissa wore. Taking notice of the round bump up under the dress confirmed what Amina had shared with her. "Please sit." Jalisa pointed to the lounge chair outside of the office.

Melissa purposely began loudly weeping, accompanied by heaving as if she couldn't breathe. Jalisa walked away to get Melissa something to drink and a box of tissues. "If there's anything else that I can get for you, don't hesitate to ask. You can just sit here until Pastor Sampson comes," Jalisa advised Melissa before walking back toward the sanctuary to see if Crystal needed anything else.

"Sister Jalisa?" Melissa feigned her unstable behavior and would do so until she could speak with Crystal and expose Nathaniel for impregnating her, and then leaving her high and dry.

Jalisa turned around slowly and mustered up a smile. She couldn't deny the ill feelings that Melissa was putting off. "Yes, what can I do for you?" she asked.

"I was just wondering if you could tell me why no one reached out to me during my absence. Isn't there a ministry that is supposed to contact members who've been missing in action for more than one Sunday? Or should I just chalk it up to the fact that I'm not a valuable vessel to this ministry?" Melissa's tears had dried, and she could feel her ghettoism slipping past her usually reserved façade.

Jalisa knew exactly what Melissa was getting at. Amina had called her immediately after the sordid center fiasco happened weeks ago. Amina was in bad shape, and she didn't feel that she should tell Crystal what was going on; however, Jalisa was the closest thing to a sister that Amina had, and they had shared many secrets in the past. Amina told her everything that Serena shared with her that day before going to the center. So it was no surprise that Jalisa could see through the fake show of emotion that Melissa put on.

That time Jalisa didn't even turn around to address Melissa, but she spoke over her shoulder instead. "Oh . . . You haven't been here?" She snickered before turning around and giving Melissa her full attention. "Your deacon should have been in contact with you during your absence." Jalisa knew that Melissa hadn't been there, and she was pretty happy about it. No one really cared for Melissa in the church because there was no visible transformation in her life according to those who were paying attention. "You can discuss that with Pastor when you all meet," Jalisa said before walking off down the hall back to her post.

Before Jalisa reached the end of the hallway, Tremaine led the way, with Crystal following behind him in the direction of Melissa. When Melissa heard soft voices coming her way, she snatched up a Kleenex and sniffled loudly. Then she pressed the tissue up against her face.

"Sister Melissa, if you will give me just a few moments to go in and get myself situated, I'll then send for you. I won't be very long," Crystal assured her. She stepped to the side so that Tremaine could open the door to her study. Crystal and Jalisa went in together before he pulled the door closed and stood guard.

Tremaine's thoughts traveled through his mind a million miles per minute as he envisioned the proposal he was ready to spring on Crystal. His forehead creased as thoughts of Serena and what she was going through made their way to the forefront of his mind. He hadn't really talked to her since the day they went over for the so-called intervention a month and a half ago.

Looking back over at Melissa, it was apparent to Tremaine that something wasn't quite right with her. Studying her posture and her demeanor mirrored the patients who were admitted to the psych ward in the hospital. He'd seen it many times before during his transports of other patients to the floor designated for mentally ill people in the hospital.

Melissa sat, ignorant of Tremaine's observation of her. She picked her nails until they began to bleed. Her teeth gritted and pain showed on her face, but she didn't stop. She wondered what Crystal and Jalisa were discussing in there because it had been about fifteen minutes since they went and shut the door. She felt that Crystal didn't like her, and with what she was about to do, she expected to begin receiving hate mail, and maybe even get kicked out of the church. Being ex-communicated was the least of Melissa's concerns, however. It was her goal that if she had to leave, then Nathaniel wouldn't be too far behind her.

Finally the door opened to the office and Jalisa motioned for Melissa to come in. "Pastor Sampson is now ready to meet with you." Jalisa nodded to Tremaine, and he left the hallway.

"Come on in, Sister Wright," Crystal said, paying attention to detail. She looked at the way the dress fell over her slightly protruding belly. The hair stood up on the back of her neck as she fast-forwarded the meeting. "Please forgive me for the time I needed to take to grab a li'l snack and drink some juice to keep my strength up until I can get a real meal." Crystal met Melissa at the door and beckoned her in. Once she'd crossed over the threshold, Crystal dismissed Jalisa and offered Melissa one of the wing-backed chairs to sit down on. She moved toward her desk and took her seat.

"Pastor, I know that I may seem a little unlike myself," Melissa said looking down at her fingers which were bloodstained and searing with pain. Sliding her hands beneath her pocketbook, Melissa couldn't look at her pastor in the eyes. Fear set in, and she wondered if she was doing the right thing after all. She had convinced herself that she needed to reveal to her spiritual leader what had happened. It wasn't fair for Melissa to have to raise a baby on her own when Serena was getting the house, baby, *and* Nathaniel.

Crystal pushed back in her chair, and then immediately sat erect, as if on guard. She figured that she'd better sit up so that when she busted whatever that wolf in sheep's clothing was ready to expose that she'd be on guard in handling it. Folding one hand across the other and leaning forward onto her desk, she asked, "Melissa, what is it that brought you to my office today?"

"Well, let's see . . . Where should I begin?" Melissa looked in Crystal's direction, trying to gauge her expression by her stiff demeanor. When no answer came from Crystal, Melissa took that as her cue to get on with her reason for being there. She felt Crystal's stare as it smacked Melissa across her cheek. Her nerves became unhinged, and Melissa burst out crying uncontrollably. Before Melissa knew it, her mouth flew opened, and she had laid all of Nathaniel's and her secrets on the desk in front of their pastor.

Crystal struggled to hide her surprise at what she'd heard. She thought back over the last few weeks and remembered that Melissa hadn't been in church, and Serena had been absent as well. Crystal's eyes dropped down to Melissa's midsection, and it all made sense to her then.

"You're pregnant by Brother Nathaniel?" Crystal asked in disbelief. As if a lightbulb went off in her head, Crystal snapped her fingers, and then placed her hands in her lap.

Melissa seemed to lose her bravado that she'd displayed earlier. Her confidence had left her high and dry, leaving fear in its wake. She kept her eyes downcast and shifted in her seat, wishing that she could disappear, but instead, she answered, "Yes, Pastor, that's what I said."

Things were on shaky ground between Nathaniel and Serena, not only because of the recurrence of the cancer and the grim prognosis, but because her son-in-law stooped to such ratchetness and had an affair with Melissa, of all people. Once Crystal was able to coax her voice out of hide-and-seek, she asked Melissa if there was anything else that she'd wanted to share with her. It was imperative that Crystal get that woman out of her office before she laid unholy hands on her.

Melissa felt a leap in her belly, and it wasn't from the anxiety she'd experienced just moments ago before spilling her guts to Crystal. At five months pregnant, the baby had been pressed on her bladder for over an hour. She was antsy because she needed to empty her bladder, and that was the only thing on her mind at that moment. What should have been feelings of conviction for Melissa turned out to be vindication of what she believed to be the only way she could get back at Nathaniel for hurting her, and it didn't even matter to her that Serena, who was innocent of any wrongdoing, would pay as well.

Crystal sat and contemplated what she could say to Melissa that would be of a spiritual enlightenment because she was in her flesh at this moment. What she really wanted to do was jump over her desk and beat the child down, but she couldn't do that; after all, she was a pastor. Looking around to keep from looking at Melissa in her pathetic face, Crystal got up and walked around to the other side of the office. She'd never been grateful for the expanse of the room before that day, but she knew that she'd have to repent later for complaining about her small office space.

The smug look that sat upon Melissa's sweaty face was slowly disappearing as she felt the cold draft of Crystal walking to and fro across the floor. She almost ducked because the draft was getting closer and closer to her. Afraid to move, Melissa sat stark still, as if she'd been turned into a pillar of salt. She waited for a sign that Crystal wasn't going to snap, holding her breath for as long as possible before exhaling and inhaling again. The moment Crystal sat back down at her desk, Melissa put up her pointer finger and without saying a word, left the pastor's study.

She bypassed one ladies' room in order to get as far away from Crystal's office as she could before walking to the bathroom on the far side of the church. Out of breath, Melissa huffed and puffed as she pushed her way into the bathroom. Locking herself in the stall at the far end of the bathroom, she ripped her stockings in her rush to empty her bladder. Finally sitting down, she exhaled before pulling her phone out and calling her best friend. "Trina, girl, you won't believe it but that woman was gon' kill meeee," Melissa screamed into her cell phone.

"What? Who tried to kill you, crazy? And what is that noise? Are you running water?" Trina asked, uninterested as she enjoyed the swooshing of the water on her feet as she treated herself to a pedicure at the nail spa "Please don't tell me you have done something else crazy like going back down to that center and causing a ghetto ruckus. You know this is my only day off, right?"

"Well, you'd know if you would have brought your happy hips to worship service today," Melissa said. "I needed you for support when I went to meet with Pastor Sampson. I told her all about Nathaniel and me. About the affair and the baby, so she knows that her son-in-law isn't as honorable as she thought. And, girl, she was hot. I mean, for real. She almost lost her holy walk. Ah, my bladder was on overload. Your godchild has been resting in the same spot for the last few hours," Melissa said as an afterthought.

Trina sat up straight in her chair and shooed away the young Vietnamese nail tech so that she could give Melissa her undivided attention. The woman obviously didn't understand English so she continued to trouble the water, and Trina kicked at it to splash it on her. "Oops, I'm so sorry," Trina lied as the nail tech jumped up and spoke real fast in her language, sounding like a wounded animal as she scurried away.

"Sorry about that, girl, now, tell me what happened and spare nothing," Trina said and sat back to allow the chair's automatic masseuse work the kinks out of her back.

"Well, the Word was real good today. I mean it was so good that I started to feel emotional," Melissa explained before Trina interrupted her.

"Are you sure that it was the emotional high from the sermon or your hormones being jerked from one end of your uterus to the top of your chest due to being pregnant?" Trina asked, knowing good and well that Melissa never entered into the church with church on her carnal mind.

Melissa smacked her teeth as she flushed the toilet. Feeling a little calmer since leaving Crystal's office, she said, "First of all, if you're going to be sarcastic, then I can just talk to you another time. Second, I beg your pardon, I go to church to get all I can from the Word, but most of the time, those sermons just don't apply to me. Usually, I leave feeling unfulfilled, wondering why I still go to church." Melissa's explanation even left a bad taste in her own mouth.

"Uh-huh, now what happened when you told Pastor Sampson about Nathaniel, the baby, and all that?" Trina tried to rush the conversation along so that she could get back to her pedicure. The nail tech hadn't returned since she'd gotten splashed, so Trina knew that a hefty tip would be in order.

Melissa's explanation got caught in her throat, and she clicked the end button on her cell phone as she heard someone come into the bathroom. Craning her neck toward the door, she listened as the two ladies were talking. She sat still to see if she could make out what their conversation was, but she only heard their whispering and laughing out loud. Melissa didn't want anyone to know that she was there, so she stayed in the stall as still as a church mouse and waited for the ladies to leave. When the door opened, she quickly washed her hands, exited the restroom, and headed home.

Chapter 15

"Are you sure that we should be doing this?" Tremaine asked Crystal as they sat out in Serena and Nathaniel's driveway.

"We're here, aren't we?" Crystal looked at Tremaine and continued, "I've held my tongue long enough, and since my own daughter isn't going to tell me what's going on between her and Nathaniel, then it's time for an intervention." She watched Tremaine's facial expression, hoping that she hadn't upset him. Ever since Melissa came into her office with her "big secret" that she couldn't wait to blurt out, the news had been eating at Crystal. God had given her a measure of patience over the years, and usually she would wait for the news to come to her about her members, but this was her family.

"When you go in there, you need to remember not to upset Serena. Don't press too hard and don't go in with a judgmental attitude when Nathaniel enters the room," Tremaine coached her, reminding her that cooler heads would prevail.

"I've been pastoring for many years, thank you. I know how to handle God's sheep." Crystal rolled her eyes at him, suddenly wishing that he had to work that evening.

"I don't question your ability with handling the sheep of God, but this goes deeper than a church relationship. Serena's not only your spiritual daughter, but your natural daughter as well. I just want you to remember that this doesn't need to be any harder for Serena than it already is," Tremaine reminded her.

"Note taken, now, can we go inside please? I've been cooking up a storm today, and I need to get it inside before it gets cold. I don't want for Serena to feel like she has to do anything extra besides sit down and hopefully eat this good meal."

"Babe, just promise me that you won't lose yourself in there. I know that this visit is going to be an emotional one, and Serena will need for you to not do things the way you are used to doing them dealing with her. She's going to need you to listen if she feels like talking, and if she doesn't, then don't press her." Tremaine felt the need to make sure that Crystal understood what he was saying and prayed that she would take heed of it.

"Man, if you don't get on out of this car and come around here and open this door for me, then I'm going to leave you in here and go in alone." Crystal huffed and fussed to herself while Tremaine tried to give her a kiss on the cheek. She moved her head away and asked, "Are you ready to go in now?"

"I'm ready when I feel like you're ready. Before we get out of this car, I need a kiss and for you to smile. There's no need to get upset when all I'm trying to do is help you defeat the enemy. Family is off-limits when it comes to matters of the heart, and no mother wants to see her child dealing with all that Serena has on her plate." Tremaine puckered his lips and leaned over to kiss Crystal on the cheek.

Crystal didn't say anything, but leaned over to give Tremaine her cheek to kiss. She agreed with him, and she thanked God for sending him to her. It had been many years since she'd had to answer to a man, but now that she had one, she was in the right frame of mind to submit to him. "It's only a test," she'd told herself over and over as she waited for him to come and open her door.

***

Nathaniel had been sleeping on the couch for months now, and he'd gotten pretty used to it. He couldn't deny that he wished that his wife would allow him back into their bed where he belonged, but he respected Serena's wishes. His heart ached for her, and he wallowed in his shame. Looking up at the ceiling, he wondered how he'd fallen so far from grace. Tears fell from his eyes as he reflected on the first day he went to Melissa's home. Knowing that she would welcome him in, he went to her. Instead of stopping before things got out of hand, he'd become intimate with her.

The doorbell chimed, bringing Nathaniel out of his daydream. Sitting up, he wondered who could be at the door. Peeping out of the living-room window, he saw Crystal and Tremaine standing on the other side of the house carrying bags and pots. He didn't remember if Serena mentioned that they would be coming over, but nevertheless, he moved toward the door, wiping his face down before unlocking and opening it.

"Hey, what are you two doing here?" Nathaniel asked, opening the door wide and stepping back to allow them entrance into the house.

Tremaine entered first wearing a smile and a look on his face that said, "We come in peace."

"Well, your mother-in-law here thought that we could do something nice for you and Serena by preparing dinner. I hope you haven't eaten yet."

"Hey, son, I hope that we aren't intruding on anything." Crystal leaned over and gave Nathaniel a kiss on the cheek. "I know I should have called first, but I wanted to surprise you all with this here." Crystal held her arms apart with hands laden with bags.

"Here, let me get those bags from you, Mom. You aren't interrupting anything around here. Serena's in the bedroom and has been most of the day, and, well, as you can see, I've been hanging out in the living room," Nathaniel said.

"Don't you worry about anything. This evening our place is in the kitchen." Tremaine slapped Nathaniel on the back with his free hand before following Crystal.

"Well, you know where everything is." Nathaniel turned back to the living room to pick up some of the snack bags, empty soda cans, and water bottles that he'd been collecting. He didn't have to worry about Serena fussing since she'd been spending most of her time in their bedroom. He reminisced on the day he took Serena in for her ultrasound. When they shared a kiss and Serena said she'd forgiven him, he automatically thought that he would be allowed back into the bedroom. But that was the furthest thing from the truth since he'd been banned from sharing their bed once again.

The aromas from the kitchen brought Serena from her room with a smile on her face. It had been awhile since she'd last eaten, and she was ready for some good food. Floating into the kitchen, she burst with joy seeing her mother standing at the stove doing what she did best. Serena thought back to the times that Crystal would cook meals large enough to feed an army.

"Mommy, what are you doing here?" she asked, knowing that with her absence at church that Crystal was here for more than providing a hearty meal for her family.

"Hello to you, and what does it look like I'm doing?" Crystal sashayed around the kitchen with a wooden spoon in her hand. "I'm here to feed my grandbaby, of course." She used her free hand and rubbed Serena's baby bump through her wrinkled shirt that read, KEEP CALM, I'M HAVING A BABY. "Go rest yourself and I'll let you know when dinner's ready." Crystal returned to stirring the gumbo.

"Mom, did you come alone? Where's Tremaine?" Serena asked.

"Oh, you know that he doesn't allow me to go too far when there's food involved. He must be in the living room with Nathaniel. Go say hello. He'll be happy to see you," Crystal encouraged her.

"Hmm, maybe I should go and clean up some first. I mean, look at me, Mom, I look a mess." Serena ran her hands through her short hair. It had been thinning from the stress of her issues in her marriage. She needed to make a hair appointment because she'd given up on taking care of it.

Crystal prayed internally, grateful that she'd been able to keep her peace for as long as she had. For the last couple of weeks after meeting with Melissa in her office, she'd had trouble sleeping at night. During the days she'd often pick up her phone to call Serena to confront her about what she'd been told, but would always think better of it and disconnect the call. The only ones who seemed to be stable were Amina and Jonathan. Inasmuch as Crystal was still angry at Nathaniel for hurting her daughter, she knew that she needed to put her personal feelings aside and speak to God on their behalf. But for the longest time, she didn't know exactly what she would say to Him.

Chapter 16

"Do you want to know what you're having or do you want the sex of your baby to be a surprise?" the obstetrician asked Melissa.

Melissa had butterflies in her belly when it was time for her to find out the sex of the baby. She'd been nervous because she had four months before she would become a mother. Being accountable for someone other than herself was a reason to be anxious. She was happy that she could begin decorating her additional bedroom for the baby. "If you can determine the sex today, I would love to know. I'm sure that my fiancé will be happy either way as long as we have a healthy baby." Melissa wished that she could eat her lies, but she'd released them into the atmosphere, and there was no way possible to capture them.

"Okay, well, let's get started. Do you need to use the bathroom before we begin?" the nurse asked.

"Oh, I was under the impression that I needed to have a full bladder for the test," Melissa said.

"Well, upon reading your chart, it shows that you are twenty-seven weeks along. Anything further than twenty weeks doesn't require that you come in with a full bladder. The fetus is large enough as the uterus has moved outside of your pelvis area. So if you need to use the bathroom beforehand, I'll be happy to assist you to the ladies' room." The nurse smiled at her.

"No, I think I'll be okay. I'm more interested in finding out what my baby's sex will be, so a little discomfort will be well worth it." Melissa smiled and shifted her body to get comfortable.

The obstetrician moved the wand around for more than three minutes, yet she wasn't relaying any information to Melissa, which caused her to begin to worry. She watched in silence as the woman looked closer at the monitor, which was shielded from her view. Panic rose up in Melissa's throat and fear of the unknown paralyzed her.

"Miss Wright?" the nurse finally spoke and called out to Melissa.

"Is there something wrong with my baby?" Melissa had heard the nurse the first time, but was too afraid to answer, unsure of what she would be told.

"I need to show you something here on the monitor. Please look this way as it's imperative that you understand the information that I'm about to give to you," the nurse advised.

"Oh no, please don't tell me that my baby won't make it," Melissa cried.

"Miss Wright, I really need for you to calm down and let me explain what I'm seeing so that we can move forward," the nurse said in a soothing voice.

Hours later, Melissa still couldn't believe the news about her baby. She'd found out that her baby would be born with spina bifida. Melissa thought that only happened in the movies that she watched on Lifetime TV. "How could this have happened? Did the drinking do it?" she quizzed herself as she thought back on her destructive behavior over the past four months.

She sat at her computer looking over the pamphlets she was given and frantically typed in Causes of spina bifida. She blamed herself although there were no genetic links known. She cursed herself as she looked at the glass filled with wine that she poured upon walking into her house. Pulling out her cell phone, she called Nathaniel. She refused to go through the torment of their baby's condition alone.

"Come on, man, and answer your phone!" Melissa shouted as she waited impatiently. The phone rang and rang, eventually going to voice mail. "Nathaniel, I really need to speak with you. It's about our baby, and I have no one else to turn to." Picking up her glass, she sipped the wine, hoping that she would calm down. The wine had the opposite effect, however, and it seemed the more she drank, the more frazzled she became.

The words on the computer screen were blurred, but Melissa couldn't take her eyes off of the horrible truth that was plastered there. She called Nathaniel unsuccessfully twenty times, and she'd left twenty messages. By that time she was hysterical and spastic. Melissa couldn't believe that her desperation of getting Nathaniel would cost so much. She couldn't even go to the church anymore because of the shame and guilt she had. She angrily shook her head at herself and rubbed her protruding belly.

"Mommy's sorry, baby," she slurred. Trying to stand proved to be impossible, so Melissa got down on her knees and crawled over to the couch. She was able to pull herself up and lie down. Melissa felt defeated as her head pounded from the effects of the liquor, and eventually, she cried herself to sleep.

The incessant ringing of Melissa's doorbell snatched her from her deep sleep. She willed her eyes to open, but they were stuck together. Using her fingers, she pried her eyelids apart, wiped the saliva from her opened mouth, and lay there gathering her senses while the person on the other side of the door continued to press on the doorbell. Head pounding, Melissa took her time getting to the door. When she opened it, she saw Nathaniel and Trina standing there with worried looks on their faces.

"What are you two doing here?" she asked, shielding her face from the bright morning sun. She walked away from the door, leaving them both standing there.

"Girl, what do you mean, what are we doing here?" Trina screamed. "I mean, I can see why you're asking what *he's* doing here, but *you* called *me* yesterday." Trina sucked her teeth and walked into the house with Nathaniel on her trail.

"Melissa, what's going on?" Nathaniel asked worriedly. "You said something about the baby was sick or something. It was impossible to make sense of what you were trying to say due to your slurring on the phone." Once Nathaniel reached the living room, he walked over to the dining table where he saw an empty wine bottle and an overturned glass. He shoved his hands in his pockets, and his voiced filled the room. "I can't believe that you're still drinking. I thought you'd put this foolishness away." He turned to face Melissa and said, "I'm sorry that I missed your calls yesterday, but I have a lot of things going on in my own home." As he spoke, he looked around the room seeing another empty wine bottle and overturned glass. Papers and pamphlets were strewn all over the floor.

"I don't need you asking me nothing about what I do in my own house," Melissa spat back in Nathaniel's direction. "You have problems, well, *I* have problems too, and the most important one right now is the fact that the baby I'm carrying—your child and mine—is not going to be born healthy," she fumed. "Can you think about anything else but what's going on at *your* house? You have just left me to myself, and you barely check on me to see how I'm doing. I know you're upset about me coming down to the center and meeting up with your li'l wife, but I didn't get here by myself." Melissa ran her hands up and down on her swollen belly. "Now, whether you like it or not, you *are* this child's father, and I refuse to be disregarded another day," Melissa said, crying fresh tears.

Trina went to Melissa's side and hugged her. She wasn't happy with all of the drama going on in her best friend's life, but she knew that Melissa needed her more than ever. Her heart went out to both Melissa and Serena. She almost had an anxiety attack when Melissa told her about what she'd overheard regarding Serena's illness. Trina knew that Nathaniel had been going through it now that everything was out in the open. She kept Melissa lifted in prayer, as well as Serena and Nathaniel too.

"Sis, we're going to get through this. I called Nathaniel because I couldn't reach you after calling you most of the day yesterday. I knew that you'd gone in for the ultrasound and wanted to know how things went. From the looks of things around here, they didn't go too well. I'm sorry that I wasn't able to go with you and be that support system that you needed," Trina said.

Nathaniel walked around to where Melissa was sitting and took the seat across from her. He didn't like seeing her cry, and it was past time that he took responsibility for his part in the mess that he'd created. "Listen, I'm sorry about all of this. I should have never come here the first night. What happened that night should have been a wake-up call for me that coming to see you was a mistake that I shouldn't have repeated."

"If you don't mind me saying, there's enough blame to go around between the two of you," Trina said. "Melissa, I told you that nothing good would come of this. Nathaniel is married to Prophetess Serena, and you were the cause of your own deception. You connived and tried your best to do whatever you thought would bring you Nathaniel free and clear—even to the point of sleeping with him continuously in order to carry his seed.

"And, Nathaniel, you are just as much to blame as Melissa is." Trina pointed at him. "You've known for a long time that Melissa was in love with you, yet she was just something for you to do when Prophetess Serena wasn't around. I believe that you took advantage of her vulnerable state because we all know that she's in love with you. You weren't available for her needs, nor have you counted the cost of your indiscretions."

Nathaniel contemplated what Trina said, and he knew that she was right. He'd never stopped long enough to count the cost of what he was placing on the line. For that, he'd have to live with his actions for the rest of his life. He'd hurt the woman he loved the most in the world, and he'd used Melissa as a substitute for what he only desired from his wife. The realization came crashing down on his shoulders, and they slumped due to the magnitude.

Clearing his throat, Nathaniel asked, "What is going on with our baby? You were hysterical in most of the messages that you left for me. So what's up?"

Melissa was too overcome with emotion to answer. She nodded her head over toward the computer. Trina remained by her side feeling anxious about what was going on with her godchild. Nathaniel strolled over to the computer and picked up one of the pamphlets from the computer desk and began reading. Upon seeing the words, tears fell from his eyes and he dropped to his knees. He didn't think that he could take anything else, and although he didn't feel a connection to his unborn child before that moment, everything changed the moment he realized that his child would be born with the birth defect.

Trina's heart raced as she listened to Melissa's and Nathaniel's heart wrenching cries. "Is someone going to tell me what's going on?" No one spoke, so she got up and walked over to the computer desk, grabbing a sheet of paper and reading it out loud. *"Spina bifida is the most common permanently disabling birth defect."* Trina scrolled through some more of the information and began reading aloud again.

"It's saying here that there is no concrete cause of this disorder." Trina continued reading, but had to pause as her heart sank. "Wow, I've never known anyone to have to watch their baby go through this kind of adversity before their life has begun. *Spina bifida cystica occurs when parts of the spinal cord and nerves protrude through the open part of the spine.* Oh Lord, this is the most aggressive form of spina bifida, and the side effects can be . . ." Trina's voice trailed off, and she dropped the pamphlet as tears trickled down her face.

Nathaniel had recovered and walked back over to the couch where Melissa sat and reached for her hands. He looked into her teary eyes and found it hard not to release more of his own tears as the last few months flashed through his mind. "Melissa, I know there's a lot going on in both of our lives right now. One thing I have to do is ask you to forgive me. I knew what I was doing when I walked through your doors, your home, and your heart again. One thing I didn't count on was this pregnancy, and no matter what has happened between the two of us, I don't want anything to happen to our child."

Melissa didn't want to forgive Nathaniel. Not just yet anyhow. She wanted him to suffer just as he'd caused her to suffer with no regard for her feelings. There was no family that she could share her news with, no one in the church that she trusted besides Trina. After trying to sabotage Nathaniel's character to Crystal, she knew that she couldn't face her own pastor to ask for a sincere prayer. "I hear you, Nathaniel, but I'm just not ready to forgive you at this time. I feel like such a fool for allowing myself to travel that road with you. I believed that you would wake up and smell the coffee by leaving Serena. I had dreams of the day you would realize that I'm the woman for you, but you never did."

Trina collected the information and stacked it neatly on the desk. She busied herself, allowing Melissa and Nathaniel to have some privacy. After throwing the empty wine bottle away and washing up the few dishes in the sink, she returned to the living room.

"Thank you for contacting me, Trina, and, Melissa, we'll talk later." Nathaniel stood to leave. "Please let me know what I can do to support you. I will do the best that I can to be available, but remember, I am also expecting another child. Surely I don't have to tell you that Serena's my main concern right now. You can rest assured that I will be taking a more active role in our child's health care. Let me know when your next appointment is in advance. I'd like to be there."

Nathaniel turned to walk away, and no one saw his hands trembling as the tears fell from his eyes. He knew that only God could help him to navigate successfully through the mess that he'd created. Nathaniel cried even harder as he closed the door behind himself. He gripped his head, falling to his knees in despair, not caring who saw him. He prayed for God's guidance as he tried to prepare himself for the upcoming births of his children.

Chapter 17

Serena had finally gotten tired of skipping out on church due to her embarrassment of Nathaniel's infidelity with Melissa. She was sure that the whole church knew what had happened, and she didn't want others pitying her due to what she was going through. Serena finally had to come clean with her mother about what had been going on between her and Nathaniel when she came over to fix dinner that night.

Crystal didn't hesitate to let Serena know how Melissa acted after church on that Sunday. Serena couldn't do anything but shake her head at the pathetic woman even as she remembered how Melissa acted out down at the center that day. When Crystal asked Serena why she hadn't said anything about what was going on, she broke down crying. She just didn't think there was a benefit in talking about anything that would cause her stress.

Serena begged Crystal not to be too harsh on Nathaniel. She'd explained to her that she'd forgiven him for what he'd done and even took some of the responsibility in pushing him away. She let her mother know that she'd been hard to deal with and talk to when she'd initially found out about the recurrence of cancer. Serena believed that Nathaniel's heart still belonged to her, regardless of what was designed to tear their marriage apart.

Walking by the floor-length mirror in the bedroom, Serena stopped in front of it to examine herself. She turned around slowly, taking in her baby bump of four and a half months. Sadness swept over her as she paid attention to the evident weight loss, dark circles under her eyes, and her thinning hair. Placing her hand on her neck and tracing the length of the jagged scar with her pointer finger, Serena remembered her first bout with cancer. She wished that she could wipe the feeling of doom away, but the feeling settled in the pit of her belly. It wouldn't take much more for her to give up. Her bottom lip quivered.

Nathaniel watched Serena from the door, and his heart galloped in his chest. He longed to go to her and hold her. Serena was still the most beautiful woman he'd ever seen. When he looked at her, he didn't see her sickness, and he didn't see how frail she looked. Watching Serena in all of her natural glory made Nathaniel want to make her feel secure with him again. Against his better judgment, he walked up behind her and gently pulled her into his grasp.

He held onto Serena as if she were his anchor keeping him from drowning. He wrapped his hands around their baby and kissed the side of her neck. Caught off guard when she felt Nathaniel's strong arms wrap around her, instead of flinching, Serena welcomed his touch. They hadn't had an intimate moment since that afternoon at the doctor's office after her ultrasound. Serena wasn't sure if their connection was purely instinct or genuine until she felt Nathaniel turn her around to face him and placed his lips on hers. The indecisiveness Serena had been feeling melted away as she caved into the attention that she'd been denying herself for so long.

"Serena, baby, I love you so much. I know that things haven't been good between us for a while now, but I'm committed to rebuilding your trust in me if you'll allow me to. I miss you, baby. I miss kissing you, holding you, and making love to my wife. Please let me back in," Nathaniel whispered in her ear.

Desire leaped into Serena's loins as Nathaniel's hot breath caressed her ears and traveled down her neck where his lips followed, planting soft kisses there. He'd ignited minifires everywhere he kissed her skin. Serena's head rolled back as a feeling of nostalgia took over, and she momentarily lost herself in thoughts of happier times. She remembered when their love for each other was requited. The reality of their current situation slammed into her moment of complete peace, causing her to move abruptly out of Nathaniel's reach.

Serena turned around and spoke to the man who represented betrayal, pain, and love. "I've forgiven you; isn't that enough?" She gasped, trying to catch her breath and desperately fighting to quell the fear in the pit of her soul. "I can't do this to myself or to us. Maybe you should go to Melissa. She's healthy, and she loves you. Nathaniel, she can give you more time than I can. I'm dying, I'm *dy-inggg!*" Serena bellowed as she dropped to her knees in despair.

Nathaniel ran to her side and cupped her in his arms, breaking her fall just as he always had. He picked her up off of the floor and laid her on the bed that they used to share. She held on tight until she felt him lower her onto the satin sheets that fondled her bare skin. Nathaniel wasn't sure if Serena would submit to his attempts at lovemaking, but he was up for the challenge. Determined to connect with his wife caused Nathaniel to overlook the questions in her eyes and become one with the love of his life, praying that this would take them in the right direction.

Three weeks had passed and the Jackson household seemed to be on its way to reconciliation. Nathaniel had shared with Serena the news about Melissa's baby and the possible defect the baby would more than likely be born with. Whatever feelings of anger she'd felt toward Melissa vanished, and she'd earnestly sought God on Melissa's behalf. She couldn't imagine what Melissa was feeling or going through, and she'd wondered if Melissa's pain was like hers. It took some time, but after struggling with her feelings of wanting to hate Melissa, Serena had finally come to the realization that it wasn't the baby's fault that his or her mother was just a trifling woman who lacked self-discipline and respect. Serena had finally gotten her appetite back and was eating full meals, which had improved her countenance. Her shine was back, and she felt lighter than she had in previous months.

The next morning, Nathaniel hesitantly walked into the kitchen to let Serena know that he needed to go with Melissa to her prenatal appointment. Tilting his head to avoid Serena's watchful eyes he said, "Babe, I've got to head out. I promised Melissa that I would be more involved with her prenatal care. She has an appointment this morning." Nathaniel looked around nervously while patting his pants pockets as if he were looking for his car keys.

He paced aimlessly around the kitchen with mixed emotions coursing through him. Looking at Serena eating her breakfast, he asked, "Baby, are you going to be all right with this?" Doubt was written all over his face. It was a struggle talking to Serena about another woman, especially the woman he was having a child with outside of their marriage.

"I'm going to be all right. I can't lie and say that I don't feel some kind of way about my husband going to be with another woman whose child she's carrying that belongs to him." Serena turned to face Nathaniel, rubbing her baby bump. "I mean, this whole scenario is really awkward, don't you think? One thing is for certain, and that's I know that God still lives in me because He's the only reason I'm able to have this conversation with you. I'm sure that there will be many more to follow this one, and I'm just praying that the good Lord will give me the strength to remain a good Christian and not snap out on both of y'all," she said matter-of-factly.

Emotions were high as Serena continued talking. "I'm sitting here with my belly sticking out about as far as Melissa's and come to find out that we are both on the verge of losing out. More than likely I won't be around to see my child grow up and Melissa's baby is sick already . . ." Heaviness swept through the kitchen and settled onto Serena's shoulders.

Nathaniel stared at Serena with tears in his eyes. He was afraid to move, speak, or even breathe, not knowing if he did either of the first two another setback in his marriage might occur. He walked over to Serena, pulling her up from where she sat at the table with tears in her eyes. "Baby, I'm *so* sorry for all of this." Nathaniel hugged Serena and apologized profusely. "I don't know what I was thinking when I asked you if you would be okay with me going to be by Melissa's side. All of this is a twisted mess, and it's my fault." He pulled her to him tighter, and when he didn't feel her reciprocate his embrace, he looked upward and mentally petitioned God for help.

"Nathaniel, I can't lie to you and say that all is well, but this is going to have to be okay. I knew that you were going to have to go with Melissa today, but I dreaded the moment when you would leave home to go and take care of another woman." Serena pulled back from him and looked into his teary eyes. "While never in a million years did I think that this would be my lot in life, I just have to get used to the fact of having to share my husband with another woman."

Nathaniel held Serena at arm's length and returned her stare. "Baby, you don't have to share me with anyone. I don't want for you to ever worry about me betraying you again. I'm fighting to regain your trust. I won't digress and return to what God has delivered me out of. You are the love of my life, and I was a fool to betray what we have for a dirty deal with the devil. I need for you to tell me you trust me, baby, *please*." Nathaniel's heart raced a mile a minute as he awaited Serena's reply. The quiet held a pregnant pause, and he didn't realize he was holding his breath, hoping that Serena wouldn't allow the lies of Satan to cloud her judgment concerning them.

Serena wanted desperately to believe the words coming from her man's mouth, but there was a twinge of doubt and the realization that even with honorable intentions, Nathaniel had failed them before. She didn't want her words to betray her true feelings and instead, just lay her head on his chest, listening to his heartbeat. While listening, she imagined their hearts dancing in sync with each other. Both were fearful of the unknown but refused to speak the words of unbelief into the atmosphere.

"I promise, baby, I'll be back as soon as I can. My only concern is my unborn child, and even though I know you're not asking me not to play an active role in my child's life, if I have to reassure you every time I walk out of the door that my heart, desires, and allegiance is to you and our family, then that's what I'll do. I need to get out of here since the appointment is at noon." Nathaniel kissed Serena atop her head before pulling his keys out of his pants pockets and grabbing his wallet off of the countertop before leaving the house.

Serena's heart felt like it had left her chest and crashed onto the floor when the door closed. She wanted to run to the door and beg Nathaniel not to go, but she knew that she couldn't do that. Walking into the living room, she sat down, wiping her sweaty palms on her pajamas and held her hands up to the Lord in surrender. For the first time in a long time, Serena prayed hard and began to travail in the spirit. Burdened and bound when she went to God, she didn't move until she felt a release from her Heavenly Father.